Roden Berkeley Noel

A modern Faust and other Poems

Roden Berkeley Noel

A modern Faust and other Poems

ISBN/EAN: 9783743377257

Manufactured in Europe, USA, Canada, Australia, Japa

Cover: Foto ©Andreas Hilbeck / pixelio.de

Manufactured and distributed by brebook publishing software (www.brebook.com)

Roden Berkeley Noel

A modern Faust and other Poems

A MODERN FAUST

AND OTHER POEMS

BY

HON. RODEN NOEL

AUTHOR OF

"A LITTLE CHILD'S MONUMENT," "HOUSE OF RAVENSBURG," ETC.

LONDON

KEGAN PAUL, TRENCH & CO., 1, PATERNOSTER SQUARE

1888

TO MY DEAR FRIEND

HORATIO FORBES BROWN

I DEDICATE THIS BOOK.

CONTENTS.

A MODERN FAUST.

PREFACE.

It has naturally been with no presumptuous desire to enter into any kind of competition with the great Elizabethan, or the great German Master that I have given to my poem the name of "A Modern Faust." But, seeking to pourtray a denizen of our modern world with nature and aspirations somewhat similar to those of that semi-mythical and representative Personage, I thought it not unfitting to give him the same name. For there exists a cycle of Christian mythus, semi-historical, semi-legendary, which embodies certain ideas and ideals especially pertaining to the Christian era, and which may, as it appears to me, advantageously furnish such a quarry of material for the Christian poet as the grand, familiar stories belonging to the Heroic Age of Greece—the Tale of Troy Divine, of Pelops' Line, the House of Laius, and Prometheus—furnished to successive poets in Greece. These may be handled (within certain

limits) according to the idiosyncrasy of the writer
and the special requirements of his own day, their
subject matter being essentially human and permanent. To this order of Christian mythus belong
the cycle of Arthurian romance, Faust, Tannhäuser,
and Don Juan. My own object, however, has been
to write a poem dealing with conditions and problems which must press, in one way or another, upon
the most sympathetic, thoughtful, and sensitive among
ourselves; to pourtray a sorely tried and divided
nature, keenly alive to human suffering, as well as to
the speculative difficulties peculiar to our day and
generation, arising from the conflict between science
and accepted creeds; unable, moreover, to acquiesce
in current solutions or panaceas, confidently pro-
pounded for the ills that afflict humanity—a nature
itself disorganized and enfeebled by internal dis-
sensions, through the warfare of higher and lower
selves. I have likewise endeavoured to suggest a
certain reconciliation and harmony ultimately attained
by him. It has, therefore, been with realities, rather
than titles, that I have been concerned; yet to such a
delineation the familiar name of Faust seemed not
altogether inappropriate. Though considering its
now formidable literary associations, remembering

Marlowe and Goethe, who can repress a certain feeling of trepidation in thus invoking so venerable a
name, lest he should be overtaken by the fate that
was said to have befallen rash and presumptuous
magicians, torn in pieces by the potent spirit whom
they could summon, but not control?

In the generation immediately preceding ours, it
would have been plainly impossible to introduce that
supernatural element essential to the " Faust " legend,
and yet make the hero a modern. Upon this neither
Goethe ventured, nor Byron in *his* Faust, which is
Manfred. Even Hamlet is assumed to pertain to a
very remote age, though he actually belongs to
Elizabethan England. But the recent revival of interest among ourselves in what is termed "occult
lore" has rendered such a representation perhaps less
shocking and incongruous than it would have seemed
formerly. My Satan, however, is chiefly, though not
entirely, the man's own worse self. And those who
are still certain that there is nothing in heaven or
earth undreamed of in their philosophy may chari-
tably reflect that, after all, the whole phantasmagory is
intended to pass in a dream ! *

* The incidents embodied in the section " Earth's Torture-
Chamber," I am sorry to say, really happened, though, to soften

the horror, I have modified them in detail. They were cases dealt with by the excellent Society for the Prevention of Cruelty to Children. Some other incidents also, illustrative of mischance and suffering, are founded upon fact. I have used prose where it seemed appropriate to my subject-matter.

SUMMARY.

————◦∘◦————

PROLOGUE.

BOOK I.—INNOCENCE.

Religion.

BOOK II.—DOUBT.

Adventure, Love, Loss—Lost Lamb.

BOOK III.—DISORDER.

CANTO I.—Earth's Torture-Chamber—The Holy Innocents—My Little Ones.

CANTO II.—The Flesh—Triumph of Bacchus—Siren Song—Pan.

CANTO III.—The Ascetic Life—Devotion—Speculation—Lyric of Thought.

BOOK IV.—DISORDER.

Prose Interlude—The World; or, The New Walpurgis Night—The World in the Church—The Palace of Art—Good Society—Respectability—Babel, and Will-o'-the-Wisp—Ragnarok—Stump Oratory—Bewilderment.

A MODERN FAUST.

PROLOGUE.

THE vision of a Pilgrimage
Made in this our modern Age
By one who went from faith to doubt,
Through all the evil rabble rout
Of mad disorder, and new lore,
That saps foundations firm before.
Many men, and many lands
He wandered over; mind expands;
The heart by loving learns to love,
And more by losing; darkly throve
Foreboding also, when the rod
He saw the oppressor wield, who trod
On human hearts, the doubt of God.
Yet, charging all on man, he goes,
In part for solace, to the shows
Of world-illusion, by fair sense
Held captive; when delivered thence,
Suffereth for that offence

B

In cloisterly, devout seclusion.
Him the importunate confusion
Following, hales from meditation,
Where, far from earthly tribulation,
He lies, with action closely furled,
Pondering the riddle of the world.
Involved in pensive solitude
The hermit may no longer brood ;
Wave-washed from his rock-island home,
Once more affronts the wandering foam.
A pretty boudoir of toy Art
Surveys, but only to depart.
World's indifference he tries,
Behind respectabilities,
Which are as walls built thick and high
To ward offence from ear and eye.
And yet his heart obeys the lure
Of sundry, who propound their cure
For social sickness ; curious mind
Blindest leader of the blind
Will follow ; but, alas ! no goal
Crowns who yield to their control ;
Long builded order fades away
From these, who to the desert stray ;
Nor hoped oasis beams upon their way.
Then, finding refuge in lone Nature,
He, wearying of her mystic stature,
Returns where poor Humanity

A MODERN FAUST.

Doth agonize, do evil, die,
On icy heights, amid the scorn
Of gods and demons, vulture-torn !
Learns at length that not alone
Fault of ours hath wrought our moan.
Whence cometh evil, who shall say,
In man, the creature of a day ?
The dumb Sphinx-Nature dooms no less
Than men, though ne'er so pitiless ;
Turns her thumbs down, votes for death.
The whole creation travaileth
With conflict, suffering, and care ! . . .
Spirits in the murk of air
Wail and whisper doubt, despair ;
Whom angels answer, to dispel
Inner night that o'er him fell.
He dared the invisible invoke,
And so the mirthful scorn provoke
Of latter day omniscience,
That doth all knowledge, save through sense,
Prohibit ; yet he deemed there spoke
Voices verily to him,
And forms unearthly, fair, or grim,
Came palpable, now pale and dim ;
Yet often hard to be divined
He found it, if to his own mind
Or theirs a thought should be assigned,
Believing he the problem solved.

By holding both alike involved . . .
Last, Devil-driven to end all,
Enveloped in Despair's bleak pall,
Love plucks him from the final fall;
Offers hope and mercy mild,
In guise of a dear little child;
With olive-leaf from forth the dark,
A dove taps at life's wildered ark.
And so the prodigal comes home,
Though not to where he wandered from.
Scarce may any wanderer find
The very place he left behind.
But he returns to faithful labour;
In Art reflecting Nature, neighbour,
And a soul whereover lay
Brooding problems of to-day,
As in a lonely mountain lake
Mirrored vapours roll and break,
Sullenly involved, unravel,
Murmur tempest while they travel.

Apollo with the Python wages
Awful warfare of the ages !
It may be the All draweth breath
From good and evil, life and death.

A dream of childly happiness,
A dream of children's dire distress ;
A vision, fain to reconcile
Powerful oppressions of the vile,

And what appears a casual slaughter
By elements of fire or water,
With Love and Righteousness, which are
More than earth, or moon, or star,
Grander than the night and day,
World-foundation old and grey.
If aught more real lie below,
It is not less than these, we know;
May only complemental lie
To their sublime eternity.

BOOK I.

INNOCENCE.

BOOK I.

INNOCENCE.

RELIGION.

A SUMMER morn, a church among the trees,
A mullioned hall ancestral, and by these
Low rural homes; a river gently flows
Through green demesnes; wide, antlered woods half
    close
Upon a village church among the leaves,
Grey-towered, grove-embowered, calm and cool;
Thereof a vision to my memory cleaves,
How rare and radiant, pure and beautiful!
Before the rustic ritual began
With music, or the priest, white-raimented,
And choir entered, glad surprise there ran
Through me to note, where shadowy arches wed,
A cherub form advancing all alone,
With golden-curled head, unashamed young face,

And air that wakes the passive cold grey stone
To silent benediction on the grace
Of moving innocence, half bold, half shy,
Advancing like a sunbeam from the porch,
With timid reverence and a laughing eye.
He glides among the monumental marbles,
Reposing warriors of his ancient line,
Stone feet upon the lion; old time garbles
Their graven story! play, war, women, wine,
Church, statecraft held, who want not, nor repine.
He looked athwart dim spaces of the church
To where his gathered folk awaiting sat,
With linked looks of encouragement.   Perchance,
In the fair gardened home at hand made late
By some mishappening light circumstance,
Dubiously laughing, he resolved to dare
The long way uncompanioned.   The child
Seemed rather born from the pure atmosphere
Of all the prayers and praises undefiled
Heart-offered here through centuries; so clear
His eyes and colour, his rich locks a mist
Of fountained gold; the sun loves nestling there;
Rude congregated men and women blest
Their heavenly visitant; the chaste cool air
Among grey spaces cherished the fair guest.
Yea, and more watchers than dull eyes behold,
From whom ethereal consecration flows,
Clothed him in armour of enchanted gold,

Molten in Love's fire, mined in hearts of those
Who face the Father.   Then low music woke
Within the bosom of the calm abode ;
The hushed wave of rapt adoration broke ;
A boy's clear tones peal forth pure faith in God.

   From a more affluent lot in life he comes,
The darling ; but in many humbler homes
Have I not found a mother, like Madonna,
The cherished burthen of her child upon her,
Or beautiful, or homely, hollow-eyed,
Pale with privation, toil-worn for her pride,
Her joy, the little ones for whom she wears
Out soul and body, shedding but few tears—
Where is the leisure for them ?—o'er the pillow
Of some sick infant, unremoving willow,
Bent day and night, how eager to fulfil
The meanest function for one lying ill !
While well-loved kindly father loves to carry
His little bare-foot Jane, or crippled Harry ;
And tiny folk will frolic in dim alley
As were it purple hill, or dewy valley ;
Will play their blithe life-drama in a mean,
Poor, walled-in, soiled apology for green,
As were it lovely park, or forest scene.
They to the monkey-crowned street-organ dance
More gay, more fair than all fine folk in France,
At court superb of their grand monarch met,
To languish through the stately minuet.

Such homes are blessed, even when cruel want
Invades, though shelter, food, and clothes be scant.
I joy to know the children's joy as common
As kindness for them among men and women.

BOOK II.

DOUBT.

BOOK II.

DOUBT.

ADVENTURE, LOVE, LOSS.

THE boy, a youth now, roved in foreign lands,
By palm and temple, over burning sands,
On camels and on horses, noting men
And manners many ; mountain, forest, glen,
Populous human hives, and alien
Taste, habit, ethnic custom, ethnic creed,
Whereby, as by the late-born Lore, a seed
Was sown of gradually matured misgiving,
If circumscribing faiths exhaust the living
Spirit of universal God indeed ?
Their niggard nourishment may hardly feed
The hunger of the human ; whose wide heart
Revolts from putting for the whole the part,
From an All-Father, who hath favourites,
Vainglory, pride, and arbitrary spites,

Revengeful jealousy ! how many bands
Are loosened while the growing soul expands !
Some wholesome, dear, familiar ; wars engage
The upheaved, rent spirit, awful wars to wage !
A lone, long conflict, doubt, and grief, and rage ! .
In holy lands, in homes of ancient faith,
He journeyed, where our sacred story saith
The dear Lord lived and died for us ; he mused
Among the fallen pillars of disused
Shrines around Hermon or Mount Lebanon,
Whence all the worshippers and faiths are gone ;
Or in the golden-columned Parthenon,
The hills of olive near Jerusalem,
Far, fair Palmyra, holy Bethlehem ;
Where silent and serene Egyptian Nile
Engirdleth Philæ, palm, and peristyle,
Nourishing Thebes and Memphis ; floating long
With moonlit sail, and oft a weird wild song
From dusky crews, where gorgeous eves illume
Sphinx, flame-y-pointing pyramid or tomb,
Storied with old-world mystic hieroglyph ;
There kings lie jewelled in the fiery cliff ;
Solemn and silent in the chambered echoing cliff.
   Then rude and strange adventures him befel
With lithe and swarthy sons of Ishmael,
Full-vestmented in rainbow hues, fierce-eyed,
In Arab tents, or where dark men abide,
In marble fountained courts by Abanar :

Behind fine lacework of the lattice are
Gazelle-limbed beauties; realms of myrrh and musk,
Where in the warmth of an enchanted dusk
The minareted Muezzin calls to prayer,
Thrillingly waking a clear starlit air,
And one from Europe, wondering to be there.
    And now beneath the whispering young palm,
Enjoying dewy evening's hushed calm,
He whispered with a beautiful lithe maid,
Who wore red flowers in her hair's dark braid;
The girl had limpid eyes, a mellow tone;
Her body girdled with the enchanted zone
Of Venus queen; clear orbs came one by one
Through darkening ether, found them dallying on;
At intervals they may behold them rise;
Only they pore on heavenlier gleams in eyes
Of one another; youth, and early love!
But Fate, with flaming sword, asunder drove,
And shut them out of Paradise.
                                        Afar,
Beyond the wave, beneath a northern star,
Once more I found him with a blonder fere,
His faithful, helpful life-companion, dear
And beautiful; who smoothed his fevered pillow,
Plucked with devoted hand from death's dim billow;
Saved him, moreover, from a direr death,
Wherein sense robs of our Diviner breath.
Who saith the heart loves once, and never more?

The youth loved twice, and both for evermore
His heart holds ; yea, the clinging tendrils twine
Round others fondly, passionately incline
To many a comrade, male or feminine.
Unto these later lovers was there born
A perfect child, fair, breezy like the morn,
All laughter, light, affection, health, and song,
Who, like a rill, danced near their path along,
But unaware fell into some abyss,
And left life songless, shadowed, reft of bliss.
Inventive leader in the nursery games,
Tender, considerate of alien claims,
Full wonderful to witness in a child !
Reflection budding in the leafage wild
Of his luxuriant joy; the parents said,
" A glorious manhood when we both have fled,
One may divine for him ; our staff and stay,
When our own buoyant strength of life gives way,
Our son shall prove to us."   In one brief year
Their living sunbeam shone no longer here !
He was no more ; the wild fate-sunken twain
Were left to wail, and yearn for him with pain
Immense, deep, unassuageable, and vain.
If ever shadowy difference involved,
His young life-shining all the cloud dissolved ;
And now their marriage-bond more binding grew
Over a little grave poor grief well knew.

LOST LAMB.

HE is gone, he is gone,
The beautiful child!
He is gone, he is gone,
And the mother went wild.
Babble all silent,
Warm heart is cold;
All that remains now
The hair's living gold!
Summer hath faded
Out of his eyes,
On his mouth ne'er a ripple
Of melodies!
O where will be joy now,
To-morrow, to-day?
O where is our boy now?
Far, far away!
Light is but darkness,
Unshining from him;
Sound is but silence,
And all the world dim!
Spring's in the air!
I feel him to-day,
Spring's in the air,
He's on his way!

Warmth in the air,
Cold in my heart,
Winter is there,
Never to part !
Snowdrop asleep in the
Loosening mould,
Crocus apeep with thy
Flame-tip of gold,
Lark song who leapest
Aloft, young and bold,
My heart groweth old, for
Joy lieth cold !

So lisped be the sweet alphabet of love ;
The lesson will be fully learned above.
A gentle saintly mother, through her blood,
Him with the germ of heavenly birth imbued ;
Later with warm and holy influence
Cherished the pure life her dear veins dispense ;
So learned he love ; fair maidens taught him now ;
Many were very kind to him, I trow.
Better he learns yet from the eternal tie
True marriage, soul and body, may supply,
And from young children ; chiefly from the love
That through life-loss well nigh to madness drove :
They feared the child extinguished, and the doubt,
With tears rebellious, all light put out.
And yet I deem them sent to sorrow's school

Only for love-lore wide and plentiful.
But in that youth ancestral spirits fought
To wrest for wickedness, and bring to nought ;
He was a battle-ground for good and evil,
Like him for whom bright Michael with the devil
Contended. Ah ! sweet Heaven, a parlous fate !
And who, save God, may know the final state ?

BOOK III.

DISORDER.

BOOK III.

DISORDER.

After, the youth, to manhood grown, related
The stations of a life-experience,
In guise of vision ; fact, or parable ;
Momentous hours, firm chisel blows whereby
A character assumed decisive mould
For good or evil ; he began to tell
His proper story from the point where I
Relinquish now ; the whole in guise of dream,
Scenes pregnant with a life-compelling power,
Or symbolizing steps in a career ;
And these the well-remembered words he spake.

CANTO I.—EARTH'S TORTURE-CHAMBER; THE HOLY
INNOCENTS.

HE said, " The vision before all will show
What branded deep into my heart world-woe. . . .

A little boy runs hurrying to school,
When lo ! a toyshop very beautiful !
The broad glass front shows every kind of toy,
Just fit to take the fancy of a boy.
He pauses ; looks ; he sees some spinning tops :
O drowsy humming when it whirls ! then flops
Down after many giddy drunken reels !
How has he longed for one !—Ah ! now he feels
Two pennies in his pocket,—the school fees !
He may not buy, he knows full well, with these !
And yet withhold not your commiseration,
Ye elder folk, who have yielded to temptation !
An impulse urged him, scarce controllable ;
He is a little child ! be pitiful !
Unless ye ne'er yourselves have been to blame.
His father, (irony bestowed the name !)
Being himself without a single sin,
Resolved to let all hell loose, and so win,
If may be, this most evil child of his
From such ineffable debaucheries.
He flogs this feebleness with furious strength
Of a brute's bulk full-fed, until, at length
Run down, it craves recruitment from a drink
Of fire at some street-corner ; see him sink,
The boy, stripped bare for beating, on the bed,
Moaning in anguish ! but his childhood led
Him, like a fairy, to forgetfulness ;
For in the interval of sharp distress,

Diverted he may note a spider dart
Down the fine web it wove with subtle art
To whirl a fly within the silken toil,
Where it may leisurely devour the spoil.
Yea, any other trifle, that can catch
The light attention, he may feebly watch,
Albeit half-whimpering, for yet he feels
Dull inextinguished aching of the weals.
The outer scene may merciful beguile
From him a tearful, poor, bewildered smile,
Alluring flexile fancy from the rod,
Wherewith the 'father' plays at angry God,
Enacts rehearsals of the 'love' of Heaven,
Or that Supreme Assize; till devils seven
Return with the tormentor; at the Frown
That enters the torn victim cowers down,
Praying, with prayers that might have moved a stone,
Forgiveness; he will do so never more!
Yet with red rope-thongs every bruise and sore
The tyrant lashes.   Then such wild wind-wails
Are heard, that even dull Indifference pales,
Shaking the door, though vainly; the dread clamour
Is drowned now when, with handle of a hammer,
The ruffian strikes his own child on the head,
Until he falls in swoon, or haply dead.
And God doth not shake in the shuddering wall,
To bury what must hurl to fatal fall
Love, justice, mercy, here and everywhere

Swooning in dumb renouncements of despair,
Or sinking to foundationless abysses
Of thought-confounding chaos—where one misses
At least the spectacle my soul beholds,
The world-wide spectacle, alas! that holds
Fiends thronged in earth's red amphitheatre,
Attentive to the sanguinary stir,
And sniffing gloatingly the cruel steam
Of torture and oppression; with fierce gleam
Infernal of hot glittering eyes they watch
The unending human tragedy; to snatch
Maniacal, malformed joy in some den,
Where deeds, beast-banned in savage mountain-glen
Assault, insult, the light by being born.
Prisoned in brothels, helpless and forlorn,
Ah! God, the very babes, for worse than death,
Are pinioned by tyrants, with rank breath
Of moral plague infected, yea, deep dyed
Their lamb-white souls and bodies; crucified
Their clean flesh, only that they may subserve
The orgasm of a flaccid satyr's nerve;
While panders whom the hoary goat can pay
Batten upon Christ's little ones for prey!
Ah! thought to turn a young man old and grey!
Their parents sell them—it is done to-day.
    Now while I stand within the room,
And wring my hands above the piteous doom
Of this poor murdered child, fallen pale and still,

A mere inanimate heap, at the curst will
Of Tyranny, the vile, plague-spotted place
Teems thick with shapes of manifold disgrace
Ineffable; they breathe in the murk air,
Like maggots in a carcase; coiling there
Over each other, thronging like pale worms,
That interlacing shake misshapen forms
In horrible jubilation; hear them hiss—
'*Do you believe in God, fool! after this?*
See yonder spider at his ease devour
The impotent winged insect in his power!'
And yet, I gasp in answer, white and wan,
'*Charge upon all the wicked will of man!*'
One chuckling discord from the fearful clan
Resounded, a thin, evil shadow-laughter;
I shuddered, fainted—and the scene changed after.

            Ah! now I roam
        . To a yeoman's home;
            Meadow-bounded,
            Flower-surrounded!
            From year to year
            Inhabit here
            Well-thought-of people,
            Anigh the steeple;
            Pledged ne'er to drink,
            They frugal sink

In a bank for savings
The yield of slavings,
A hoarded thrift,
And for soul-shrift
Are oft at chapel;
They pile the apple
In yonder loft,
Manure their croft,
With cart in byre,
With hens in mire,
A horse in stable,
Good food on table,
And soft grey wings
In a mossy roof,
While robin sings
On a fence aloof,
A paradise,
With ne'er a vice,
Verily
The place should be ! . . .
But *is* that cell
In the gaol of hell,
Where (sight appalling !)
One saw crawling
Babes span long,
Who had done no wrong,
Save to inherit
Eve's demerit,

And not have been
Washed quite clean
By Church's chrism
From Serpent-schism.
For as little reason
(But I talk treason !)
Some babes on earth
Are seared from birth
With a brand of doom,
To which the tomb
Were mercy mild,
Pure, undefiled ;
Nor old divine,
Nor the Florentine,
Ever invented worse than this
For his own, or God's own enemies !
The house is haunted
By an apparition
Of a little child ! . . .
Hallucination !
An evil dream ! . . .
And yet 'tis there !
The very semblance
Of a little child
Upon the stair,
The bones protruding,
Pale skin and bone ;
His face a fever,

A famine glare
In pits for eyes.
The skeleton
Hath a load to carry,
A heavy load,
Two flat irons,
One half his weight :
Up and down
The old wooden stair,
All through daylight,
And half through night.
Up and down
The phantom flits,
Tramps with a load,
It scarce can carry. . . .
Ah ! when to sleep ?
For never rests he
From that vain labour,
Save to stumble,
Or fainting fall,
Or when a boy
(One said a brother),
Shares crusts with him
In secrecy ;
Or when the woman,
At ease below
(The father's wife),
Unlifesustaining

Meagre morsels
Doles for food.
Nay, nay, 'tis living!
And all too true!
The boy hath taken
A hunch of bread;
And now she beats him
With rods of thorn;
(The Lord wore thorn!)
He drops the irons,
Outworn at last;
(The Lord so fainted,
When He bore the cross.)
And now inflaming
With an evil salt
The old raw wounds,
She flogs again.
Such deeds were done
In days long dead,
For the glory of God,
At God's command.
I know! I know!
Ineffable orgies
Of the carnival
Of human crime
Are old as time!
Yea, uncommanded
By God the Lord,

Who doth them now?
If uncommanded
By God the Lord,
How do them now?
The wife, reclining
In a warm armchair,
Darns diligently;
Anon she feeds
A sleek furred cat.
The man, the father,
Luxuriously
Inhales, and blows
The curled blue cloud,
And lets her murder
His only child.
He sees and hears
The living ghost
Of his only son
Tramp up and down,
And sleeps at night,
Nor dreams of it.
The demon woman
Benumbs the man,
While God alloweth
The vital air
For a human soul,
Belief in love,
The love of love,

With the breath of life
For a human body,
To be slowly drawn,
Sucked forth from it,
And makes no sign ?
The child's dead mother
Makes no sign !
Ah ! that the mother
May be dead indeed,
And may not know !
This is a child, sir,
A child indeed, sir,
Like yours, like mine ! . . .
See, now he dies ;
One certifies
' A natural death !' . . .
Listen ! low convulsive laughters
Awaken old worm-eaten rafters !
Some mutter, ' *Do you now believe in God ?*'

Once more a mean room in the huge dim city !
No fire, no food, no medicine, no water,
No sheet, no blanket, and no coverlid !
A sick child on a pallet left to starve
Between bare walls ; the wind bites keen with frost.
Alone in London !   Dismal Nights and Days,
Dumb warders, alternate their kindred gloom
Grimly by her death-bed, indifferent.

—Days, long lone intervals of demi-darkness,
Whose are hoarse cries, foot-trampings, and far wheels;
Ah! never any kindly voice for her,
Meaningless murmurs, unconcerned for her;
Nights of ear-ringing, terrifying silence,
Save for some drunken ditty of sodden harlot,
A windy flare of sallow flame without—
Unsoothed, untended, and, ah! God, unloved!
Her scant frock, faded cotton; while the pair,
Whom men name 'father,' 'mother,' at their fire
Feed, warmly clothed, unheeding, near, beneath her;
Who cannot turn herself upon the bed,
Her bones protruding, lying upon her sores.
There comes no comfort, and no care, no kiss,
No drop to drink, nor crumb from the full table
Of these, who want their own child buried, where
An elder mouldereth, whose fate was hers.
    In these well-fended carcases a hollow
Gapes where the tenderest of all hearts should be,
A parent's heart—the devil did this for jest—
Their child would love them if they would allow her!
Wealthy must they be who can toss back love,
And spill, or spurn it as a common thing!
The child had one strange friend, a folded rag,
Of which she made a pet for lack of dolls;
She communed with it daily, and at night
Her wasted cheek lay over it; she named
It *Tatto*, lavished all her heart on that,

Because none other wanted her poor heart.
And when the rude, hard undertaker came,
He laid the cold, unkempt, dishevelled head
Upon the small soiled fetish of a rag,
Inside the coffin; for he found it clasped
In her thin hand what time he took her measure
For burying; to his mate he only said—
'Poor little thing! we'll put this in with her!'
His was perchance the only kindness shown her,
Less orphaned in her death than in her life.
Surely he gave his small cup of cold water! . . .
Ah! God! ah! God! art Thou but a fair dream
Of our distracted pity? couldst not find
For solace of this child, to fill the place
Of these most fearful beings, masquerading
In guise of man, one common human heart?
For she was all ungirt with mystic light,
That panoplies the martyred patriot,
Or saint; fair well-sustaining effluence
Of the soul's inner hidden Holy of holies;
The glory that illumines the lone steep
Of causes championed to the uttermost,
Irradiating subterranean
Dark dungeon, paling the full jewel-blaze,
And cloth of gold in courts and thrones of kings.
This youth is one dependence, wants our help
As emptiness wants filling of the air.
Parents to fail their little one! As though

The sun should fail the morning, or the rain
Fail wells, and rivers, and the dancing spring!

How clear the auroral atmosphere
Of dewy, childly joy!
But children close their fans for fear
At shadow of annoy,
And you may shut them from their light
With your huge bulk of ghostly night;
So soon as you withdraw your shadow,
They will re-open on the meadow,
And with a sunny laugh
How cheerily will quaff
Your newly shining smile
In a very little while!
Ah! they will kiss the very hand
That dooms them to a loveless land,
Or scars them with a cruel brand.
What a curse that kiss will be
To guilty souls, awaking in Eternity!

MY LITTLE ONES.

Ah! little ones! my little ones!
When will your sorrows end?
We deemed you daughters, deemed you sons
Of our Eternal Friend!
Yet ever tears of blood we bleed
Above your bitter mortal need!

I deem that it may be your part
To break, and melt the world's hard heart :
And when ye know, ye will rejoice ;
In Heaven, will you give your voice
For earthly pain, your own free choice?
In the life that follows this,
Will you, with your forgiving kiss,
Pile the saving coals of fire
On cruel mother, cruel sire ?
Little ones, my little ones,
Ah ! when will be the end ?
We deemed you daughters, deemed you sons
Of more than earthly Friend !
We want you fair, and hale, and strong,
Full of laughter, mirth, and song ;
For when we hear you weep and moan,
Our Lord is shaken on His throne !
If later years be dull and sad,
Leave, O leave the children glad !
Little ones, my little ones,
However all may end,
Earth may fail, with moons and suns,
But never, Love, your friend !
For Jesus was a little child,
And God Himself is meek and mild.

Nay, but there came here no deliverer,
No glance, no tone of kind alleviation ;

The neighbours are aware of the slow murder;
And yet none knocks to save; arrests the man.
Encountered in the workshop, in the street,
None shakes from him the torturer's red hand;
But loungers lounge, and merry-makers hurry;
While floors, and walls, and ceilings keep the same
Abominable immobility,
As when some mother's burning heart of hearts
Bleeds, breaks above the interminable pain,
And slow extinction of her youngest-born.
The sunlight, soiled with coming to these courts,
Lurid, or livid, day defiled with smoke,
Faint moonlight, timid starlight, went and came;
They saw, or saw not; went, and came unheeding!
All these contemplate with the same dull stare
The widow's only son restored to her
From Nairn's cold bier by Christ, and Clytemnestra,
The baleful woman, with her false feigned smile,
Snaring the hero in her toils for slaughter!
    Then mocking spectral tones assail mine ear—
'*And do you now believe in God, good sir?*'
I sobbed, 'Charge all on the free will of man,
Or on our old ill-builded polity,
Social extremes, our ignorance!'   Mine eyes
Fell on the father deep in a learned book,
'On Floating Germs,' by our great physicist;
Fell also on rare coleoptera,
Framed, under glass, hung spitted on the wall.

. . . So, shuddering at the loathly cachinnation,
That shook the room, I reeled to outer air,
My brain that teemed with burning characters,
Wiped clean now to brute vacancy—perchance
For respite from the horrors. . . .

Canto II.—The Flesh. Triumph of Bacchus.

"Then I came
To a lit palace in a lordlier quarter
Of this great builded province, till it seemed
I, entering the vestibule, heard warbled
A song, as of a siren warbling low,
Who lulls, inhales, and breathes away the soul.

Siren Song.

"Here are bowers
    In halls of pleasure,
    Flushed with flowers
    For love or leisure ;
    Breathes no pain here,
    Theirs, nor yours,
    All are fain here
    Of honeyed hours ;
    Here in pleasure
    Hide we pain,

None may measure,
Nor refrain ;
Beauty blooming,
And flowing wine !
Yonder glooming
Here Love-shine !
Breathes no pain here,
Theirs nor thine,
O remain here !
Low recline !
In Love's illuming
Woes all wane,
Of Beauty blooming
All are fain !
O remain here !
Lo ! Love shining
After rain !

The air faints with aroma of sweet flowers,
Marrying many-tendrilled labyrinths
Dew-diamonded a harmony of hues ;
And some are flushed like delicate fair flesh
Of smooth, soft texture ; delicate love-organs
Impetalled hide, depend their fairy forms ;
Ruffled corolla, pitcher, salver, cell,
Dim haunts of humming-bird, or velvet moth ;
Doves pulsate with white wings, and make soft
    sound.

Such was the floral roof; flowers overran
In lovely riot ample, mounting pillars,
Emergent from full bowers of greenery,
Water and marble, lily, water-lily,
Columns of alabaster, and soft stone,
That hath the moon's name, alternating far
Innumerable, feebly luminous.
A mellow chime dividing the lulled hours
Embroiders them with fairy tone fourfold;
And we were soothed with ever-raining sound
Of fountains flying in the warm, low light
Of pendent lamp, wrought silver, gold, and gem,
Rich with adventure of immortal gods.
Fair acolyte waved censer, whence the curled
Perfume-cloud made the languid air one blue,
And linen-robèd priest on marble altar
Made offering of fruit to Queen Astarte.
  Behind half-open broidery of bloom
The eye won often glimpse of an alcove
In floral bower, ceiled over with dim gold;
There velvet pile lay on the floor inlaid
From looms of India, or Ispahan,
With lace from Valenciennes, with silk or satin
For coverlid; they, with the downy pillow,
Have tint of purple plums, or apricot,
Of waning woods autumnal,
Salvia, moth-fan, plume of orient bird.
And here the storied walls luxuriant

Are mellow-limned ; for lo ! Pompeianwise,
All the young world feigned of a wanton joy,
Of Erôs, Io, Hebe, Ganymede,
And all the poets tell of Aphrodite,
Or her who lulled Ulysses in her isle,
The idle lake, the garden of Armida,
And more, what grave historian hath told
Of Rosamund, Antinous, Cleopatra.
Here forms of youthful loveliness recline,
I know not whether only tinted marble,
Or breathing amorous warm flesh and blood.
　　Now from a grove of laurel and oleander,
Plum, fragrant fig, vine, myrtle, fern, pomegranate,
Recalling Daphne, or Byblos, where the Queen
Hath cave and fane anear the falling water,
And where she wooed, won, tended her Adonis,
A masque of Beauty shone ; young Dionysus
He seemed, the leader of the company,
Who lolled in a Chryselephantine car
Upon a pillow's damson velvet pile ;
An undulating form voluptuous,
All one warm waved and breathing ivory,
Aglow with male and female lovelihood,
The yellow panther fur worn negligent
Fondling one shoulder ; stealthy-footed these
That hale the chariot, one a lithe, large tiger,
Blackbarred, and fulvous, eyed with furnace-flame,
A tawny lion one, his mane a jungle.

The face was fair and beardless like a maid's,
The soft waved hair vine-filleted ; he held
Aloft with one white arm's rare symmetry
A crystal brimmed with blood of grape that hath
Heart like a lucid carbuncle ; some fallen
Over his form envermeiled more the rose
Of ample bosom, and love-moulded flank ;
The fir-coned thyrsus lying along the shoulder,
And listless fingered by a delicate hand,
The languid eyes dim-dewy with desire.

Some foam-fair, and some amber of deep tone
The company to rear of him, yet nigh,
Fawn-youths and maidens robed in woven wind
Of that fine alien fabric, hiding only
As lucid wave hides, or a vernal haze ;
But some were rough and red, and rudely hewn,
Goat-shagged, satyric ; all high-held the vine,
(Or quaffed it reeling), and the fir-cone rod ;
The fairer filleted with violet,
Anemone, or rose, Adonis-flower,
The rude with vine, or ivy ; syrinx, flute,
Sweetly they breathed into ; anon they pause,
Till Dionysus, from his car descending,
Tipsily leaned on one who may have been
That swart and swollen comrade, old Silenus,
Fain to enfold the yielding and flushed form,
Even as when the god wooed Ariadne ;
So one may see them on a vase, or gem.

Then 'Io! Evoe!' broke from all :
And from the band one whom I deemed a girl
In guise of boyhood, like some Rosalind,
Came with ahungered, lustrous eyes my way ;
The delicate neck, wave-bosom almond-hued
Emerge from silk and swansdown ; lucent hose
Cling to the ripe light limbs, and half disclose,
Luxuriant lily with a wealth of charms
Exuberant rending raiment of the sheath ;
The hair, a mist of gold, went minishing
Adown the nape ; thin shadow lined the dimple
By vermeil cheek, and under shell-pink ear.
    She, folding a fair arm around me, fain,
Lifts to my lips the ruby-mantling bowl,
And her own mouth more crimson ; then she draws
Within a shadowy nest near, an alcove
For dalliance amorous, . . .
After enjoyment vanishing. . . . A change
Was wrought in my surroundings ; and there dawned
On me mine earlier love of southern summers,
Fate-ravished from me . . . now she is another's !
A mellow, ripe, a peerless womanhood !
'Art thou then yielded to mine arms at length,'
I breathed, ' my Helen ? Helen unto me,
A purer, lovelier, Helen, but another's ! ' . . .
    She fadeth, ere I hold her . . . then the form
Of one I am bound to shield from all dishonour
With spell of beauty dominant inflames,

And paralyses reasonable will. . . .
    Now looked the mournful, dim, disordered face
Of wounded Love reproachful on the storm
In my wild-heaving spirit, as the moon,
Pale, from a cloud, upon a troubled sea :
And then, I seemed to see Love lying dead.
The child, moreover, the dear child we lost
Appeared in vision ; but alas ! the eyes,
The eyes, more terrible than all ! were turned
Away from mine, and when they fronted me,
They sought the ground ; or, veiled with his dear
        hands,
I feared they wept : I know they met not mine ! . . .
    Suddenly loud, harsh, dissonant peals of laughter
Startled and mocked me ! . . . 'Thy delirium
Conjured the vision, a mere wizard-wrought,
Illusive phantasy ! but now behold bare fact !' . . .
Lo ! I am in the chill bleared street again :
One spake—
'For you, Tannhäuser, who have seen the Christ,
Those earlier pleasure-houses are a ruin,
Nor any of you may build them !   Nay, for thee,
For thee in glamour of the Venusberg
There hides no refuge from the modern woe !
Wander abroad again ! begone ! nor linger !
I flash my sword of cherubim before
The fair wall of earth's Eden, lest returning
Ye take, and eat, and live content with earth.

Ye may not quell your proud dissatisfaction,
Nor feed the hunger of a highborn soul
With husk of sweet illusion like to these,
Nor shut your heart from any bitter cry,
Lapped in a luxury of degradation,
Rendering indifferent to alien loss ;
Anon, even fearfully athirst for pain.
And if ye dally a moment, yet beware
The unholy hell of ever-enduring fire,
That endeth only, if it end, in death,
The spell of Circe, and her transformation.
Yea, Beauty is a shadow from high Heaven ;
But emblem only, not substantial ; hold not !
O queenly soul, refuse to be a slave,
And drudge for Passion ; fondle Beauty lightly ;
Nor let her hold thee spinning with the women
Immured from the free air of stalwart deed,
From bracing airs of strong, heroic deed.
But use her for thine own high ends, O queen,
Handmaiden, and not mistress ; for remember
Beauty, who flattereth poor outer sense,
Blinds often the eternal eye within ! '
   ' Yet am I fain to reconcile demands
Both of the sense and spirit,' I replied.
   And then some choir invisible was heard,
Whose ode appeared responsive to the songs
A German, and an English poet made.

PAN.

" Pan is not dead, he lives for ever !
  Mere and mountain, forest, seas,
  Ocean, thunder, rippling river,
  All are living Presences ;
  Yea, though alien language sever,
  We hold communion with these !
  Hail ! ever young and fair Apollo !
  Large-hearted, earth-enrapturing Sun !
  Navigating night's blue hollow,
  Cynthia, Artemis, O Moon,
  Lady Earth you meekly follow,
  Till your radiant race be run ;
    Pan is not dead !

" Earth, Cybele, the crowned with towers,
  Lion-haled, with many a breast,
  Mother-Earth, dispensing powers
  To every creature, doth invest
  With life and strength, engendering showers
  Health, wealth, beauty, or withholds ;
  Till at length she gently folds
  Every child, and lays to rest !
    Pan is not dead !

" Hearken ! rhythmic ocean-thunder !
  Wind, wild anthem in the pines !

E

When the lightning rends asunder
Heavens, to open gleaming mines,
Vasty tones with mountains under
Talk where ashy cloud inclines .
Over hoar brows of the heights ;
Ware the swiftly fláming lights !
    Pan is not dead !

" Whence the ' innumerable laughter,'
All the dancing, all the glees
Of blithely buoyant billowed seas,
If it be not a sweet wafture
From joy of Oceanides?
Whence the dancing and the glees,
In the boughs of woodland trees,
When they clap their hands together,
Hold up flowers in the warm weather ?
Gentle elfins of the fur,
Flowers, Venus' stomacher,
Grey doves who belong to her,
Singing birds, or peeping bud,
Lucid lives in limpid flood,
Fishes, shells, a rainbow brood,
    If Pan be dead ?

" Naiads of the willowy water !
Sylvans in the warbling wood !
Oreads, many a mountain daughter

Of the shadowy solitude!
Whence the silence of green leaves,
Where young zephyr only heaves
Sighs in a luxurious mood,
Or a delicate whisper fell
From light lips of Ariel,
    If Pan be dead?

"Wave-illumined ocean palaces,
  Musically waterpaven,
  Whose are walls enchased like chalices;
  Gemmed with living gems, a haven
  For foamy, wandering emerald,
  Where the waterlights are called
  To mazy play upon the ceiling,
  Thrills of some delicious feeling!
  Sylph-like wonders here lie hid
  In dim dome of Nereid;
  Tender tinted, richly hued,
  Fair sea-flowers disclose their feelers
  With a pearly morn imbued,
  While to bather's open lid
  Water fairies float, revealers
  Of all the marvels in the flood,
      And Pan not dead!

"We are nourished upon science;
  Will ye pay yourselves with words?

Gladly will we yield affiance
To what grand order she affords
For use, for wonder ; yet she knows
No whit whence all the vision flows !
Ah ! sister, brother, poets, ye
Thrill to a low minstrelsy,
Never any worldling heard,
Ye who cherish the password,
Allowing you, with babes, to go
Within the Presence-chamber so
Familiarly to meet your queen ;
For she is of your kith and kin !
Ye are like him of old who heard
In convent garden the white bird ;
A hundred years flew over him
Unheeding ! All the world was dim ;
At length, unknown, he homeward came
To brethren, now no more the same ;
Then, at evening of that day,
Two white birds heavenward flew away ;
    Pan is not dead !

"Spirit only talks with spirit,
    Converse with the ordered whole,
    However alien language blur it,
    May only be of soul with soul.
    In our image-moulding sense
    We order varied influence

From the World-Intelligence ;
And if Nature feed our frame,
She may nourish pride or shame,
Holy, or unholy flame ;
Real forms the maniac sees,
Whom he cherisheth, or flees ;
Real souls the sleeper kens
In dreamland's eerie shadowed glens.
    Pan is not dead !

" Every star and every planet
  Feed the fire of Destiny ;
Or for good, or evil fan it,
  Herè, Hermes, Hecate ;
By ruling bias, and career,
To all hath been assigned a sphere,
In realms invisible and here,
Obedience, administration
For individual or nation.
Ceres, Pluto, Proserpine
Are the years' youth, and decline,
Seasonable oil or wine,
Phantasmagory yours or mine ;
And if sense be fed by Nature,
With ne'er a show of usurpature
She may feed our spirit too,
And with hers our own imbue
Ruling influence from her,

Tallied with our character;
Dionysus, Fauns may move
To revel, or the lower love,
Unrisen Ariel control,
Undine of yet unopened soul,
Fallen ghost invite to fall;
Or She, who is the heart of all,
Uranian Aphrodite, whom
The world laid in a Syrian tomb
Under the name of Jesus, She
May dominate victoriously,
 And Pan be dead!

"Whence are plague, fog, famine, fevers,
Blighting winds, and 'weather harms'?
Are sorceries malign the weavers,
Through inaudible ill charms?
Disease, confusion, haunting sadness,
Lust, delirium, murder, madness,
Cyclone, grim earthquake, accident,
In some witch-cauldron brewed and blent?
Now I see the open pit;
Abaddon flameth forth from it!
Like lurid smoke the fiends are hurled
Abroad now to confound the world!
Disordered minds
Howl, shriek, wail in the wailing winds!
 Pan is not dead!

" Whence the gentle thought unbidden,
  Resolve benign, heroic, just,
  Lovely image of one hidden,
  Higher cherished, lower chidden,
  Self downtrodden in the dust?
  Silent hand of consolation
  On the brows of our vexation,
  On the burning brows of sorrow?
  Much of all, be sure, we borrow
  For that Profound of ours within,
  From our holy kith and kin!
      Pan is not dead!

" Warmth and light from shielding, sheeny
  Wings of angels, or Athene,
  Call the Guardian what you will,
  Impelling, or consoling still!
  While if to Christ, or Virgin mother,
  Hate, greed, offer prayer, no other
  Than Belial, Mammon, Ashtaroth
  Draw nigh to hear, and answer both:
  When lurid-eyed priest waves the cross
  For slaughter, gain that is but loss
  Demons contemptuously toss!
  What though ye name the evil clan
  Typhon, Satan, Ahriman,
      Pan is not dead!

"Their bodies are the shows of nature,
   Their spirits far withdrawn from ours;
We vary in our nomenclature
For the Demiurgic Powers,
To whom high duties are assigned
In our economy of mind,
As in our mortal order; they
Lead souls upon their endless way;
From whom the tender, sweet suggestion
Arrives uncalled, unheralded,
Illumination, haunting question,
Approval, blame from some one hid,
Perchance from one we count as dead;
Our eyes are holden; they are near,
Who oftenwhile may see and hear!
By the auroral gate of birth,
In the youthful morning mirth,
At the portal of dim death
Their guardianship continueth;
   Pan is not dead! . . .

"Ah! why then shrilled in the Egæan
   The choral wail, the loud lament,
Confusion of the gods Idæan,
Dire defeat, and banishment?
When the lowly young Judæan
Dying head on cross had bent,
   'Great Pan is dead!'

Sun, and Moon, and Earth, and Stars,
Serene behind our cloudy bars,
With the Magi from the East,
Yield glad homage to the Least,
Offer myrrh, and gold, and gem
Before the Babe of Bethlehem,
   Now Pan is dead!

'Yea, before the wondrous story
Of loving, self-surrendering Man
Paled the world's inferior glory,
Knelt the proud Olympian;
Then the darkness of the cross
Enthroned supreme Love's utter loss;
Then Ambition, Pride, and Lust
Into nether hell were thrust,
And Pan was dead!
The loveliness of Aphrodite
Waned before a lovelier far,
Fainting in the rays more mighty
Of the bright and Morning Star;
(Lovely will to give and bless
Maketh form and feature less)
Young-eyed Erôs will sustain
His triumph, following in His train;
Kings conquered by One more Divine
In the courts imperial shine,
Thralls owing fealty to Him,

Who dying left their glory dim ;
Feudatories, ranged in splendour,
Sworn high services to render,
With lions, leopards, fawning mild,
And drawn swords round a Little Child !
　　Pan, Pan is dead !

" For while the dawn expands, and heightens,
　Greater gods arrive to reign,
　Jupiter dethrones the Titans,
　Osiris rules the world again,
　But in a more majestic guise ;
　Sinai thunders not, nor lightens,
　Eagle, sun-confronting eyes
　Veils before mild mysteries !
　　Balder, Gautama, full-fain
　Pay humble tribute while they wane ;
　All the earlier Beauty prone is
　Before a lovelier than Adonis !
　Till even the Person of our Lord,
　In yonder daylight of the Spirit,
　On all the people to be poured
　By the dear influence of His merit,
　Will fade in the full summer-shine
　Of all grown Human, and Divine,
　And every mode of worship fall,
　Eternal God be all in all ;
　　Pan lives, though dead !

Canto III.—The Ascetic Life. Devotion. Speculation.

"Then my dream, according to the custom of dreams, shifted utterly. Admiring, and half longing, I saw venerable collegiate buildings, with theological and philosophical libraries for learned seclusion, old-world cloister and decorous close, grey sculptured cathedral with antique tower, emblazoned pane, rolling organ, and impressive ritual—well indeed for devout and retiring souls! Shall I stay here, I thought, and save mine, by mortification, contemplation, repentance, prayer? Much have I to repent of, Heaven knows! And I did cast myself down before an altar on the pavement of that church, bitterly remorseful for past sin; hours and hours were spent in prayer, wrestling with the stifling coils of evil habit, inextricably entangled around heart and imagination, like the serpent around Laocoon, pleading with tears of blood for deliverance. Ah! how often, how often had this been! What mighty levers may be in prayer and praise, and chastened meditation! What elevating influences for mankind may linger among these grand monuments of ancestral piety, art, and religious fervour! Shall I fly from mankind, and turn monk? But, even here, should I cease to burn? Would Imagination release me, wrapped by her in a shirt of fire? Grand, stern warrior-maid, Asceticism, not of this world art thou! But evil dreams and restless longings would follow *me*, infirm of purpose, even here. Ah! saintly maiden, Principalities and Powers from yonder may yet beat down your guard, confound, infect, and fire you with that worst riot of Imagination, or deaden with malign rigidity of spiritual pride!

" But, indeed, Church and World overlap, interpenetrate. In the world may you find the very breath and spirit, essential aroma of religion, devotion to God and man, though these may be named ' Ideal,' and ' Humanity,' or not named at all, only lived for; while in the Church you may discover the World stretched out at full length, luxuriating in vain pomp and empty glory. A well-built tomb is the Church often, sprinkled decently with devoutness to make it smell sweet, slabbed imposingly with marbles of sound doctrine, correctly adjusted to one another.

"The Church! no! I can no longer submit myself to authority. Those venerable doctrines have become incredible to men and women who have tasted modern science and modern philosophy. Reason and Conscience reject them. We have outgrown the ancient creeds. I can never allow my private judgment to be subjugated by priest or book. I must find out for myself what is best adapted to nourish my own soul. The prescribed milk-diets administered by official ecclesiastical nurses I find no longer appropriate to my adult requirements.

"But here is the more secular college library! There is here more than divinity, though divinity may help too. Let me stay here, and think, and read, till I find out for myself, if that may be, the riddle of the world; or, in any case, what can be more delightful and absorbing than the search itself? How exhilarating to climb the heights of speculation alone, and enjoy with rapture the ever-widening prospect therefrom disclosed! How clear and serene the ether! How calm and still these mountains of contemplation, aloof from the Earth-Babel of confused cries, vulgar care, base lust, fevered ambition! Here would I abide, and think out for myself, helped, fortified, stimulated by ancient and contemporary wisdom, a comprehensive scheme of reason, in accord with recent discoveries, and yet satisfying the higher, permanent wants and intuitions of our common nature. Then may I find also that solution which I so ardently desire for those terrible and oppressive moral difficulties, suggested by innocent and undeserved suffering, which, remaining unsolved, may even drive a sensitive soul to madness. Ah! how far more satisfying and delightful is such a life than any which sense can offer!

LYRIC OF THOUGHT.

"I, who drained the bowl of pleasure,
Satiate, in learned leisure,
Here, at whatsoever cost,
The bowl of knowledge would exhaust;
Formidable barriers
Will assault, surmount, disperse ;
The secret of the universe
Will track home, in face of Powers,
Sworn to guard their ancient Bowers,
Wherefrom they rule this world of ours,
From profane feet of intrusion,
Overwhelm one with confusion,
Who presumes to penetrate
Where they hold their awful state,
Sworn to hide from human sight,
In the hollows of the night,
The unimagined Council Hall,
Whence they rule our earthly ball,
Where Reason would confounded fall. . . .
Good? evil? neither? more than either? Night
Involves him who demands more near, familiar
  sight ! . . .
 Standards trailed in desert dust,
Arms of mighty warrior rust ;
Amid their ruin I low lie,
Staring foiled upon a sky

Serene with azure mockery,
While a witless idle air
Whistles through the carcase there,
Which was once a warrior fair!
These corses to achieve the quest
Burned once; now baffled here they rest!
Yet my companion, more wise,
Bows before dumb destinies,
Peers content upon the ground,
Notes the soil, the pebbles round,
Sets rare beetles in a row;
'For these, at any rate, we know!
Hunt eland, or the wild gazelle,
Drink from palmy limpid well!
Fruitless longing learn to quell!
With a cordial smile advance
To embrace your Ignorance!
Warm, and comfortable here,
Shed no vain, no foolish tear!
Let this fair Capua beguile;
Heed neither Rome, nor founts of Nile!'
So spake *Know-nothing:* but the Church;
''Ware unaccredited research!
The Lord commissioned me to dole
Wholesome food for human soul;
Thou, shameless Curiosity,
Dare not irreverent to pry
With dull, unpurged, earth-ailing eye!

Lo! the appointed guardian,
Warns thee to retire, rash man!
Heaven's thunder-bolt shall cleave
Who dare approach without my leave!
I will save your soul from sinking
With burdens of unchartered thinking.'
Then some prophetic strain in air
Confirmed the counsel of despair.
' Pause, kneel, and know your natal bound;
Yonder is holy ground!
Sovran gods will only tell
What heavenly wisdom deemeth well
Weak man should know;
Bend low!
With madness they confound the man,
Who will know more than mortal can!
From them no intellect may wrest
What they have locked within their breast;
To lowly heart they will reveal
All humble, holy heart may feel;
You shall be patient, loving, mild,
Become once more a little child.
Let him who fain would learn lie still,
Inquire, and do, the Holy Will.
The arrogant, hard, reasoning mind
Darkling gropeth, bare and blind!
The chariot and horseman lie whelmed beneath the
    wave,

Multitudinous might of Pharaoh, he who proudly dravé,
With music and with banner, rich robed in morning's
    beam,
Exulting in their youth and strength, they feed the
    ocean stream !
The pomp and glory of their arms wide welter on the
    sea,
Spent foam, sere leaf, the tempest-torrent whirls im-
    periously ! '
    But I, unwarned, peered wistfully afar,
    Over dim realms of mystery that are
    Never to be explored by mortal feet,
    Nor ceased with passionate crying to entreat,
    'Unveil, O Isis ! loosen the cloud-fold,
    Even though thy visage bring me the death-
    cold ! '
    Ah ! woe for whom, brain-giddying, fascinate
    The Abysmal, and impassive face of Fate,
    All-gendering Mother of devouring Law,
    Unveileth, who may tell not what he saw !
    He stammers, dazed, unheeding stupefied
    Our wonted world, and habit, haggard-eyed. . .
    Did he behold, flashed forth in lurid light,
    Thronged lives of all swept o'er the abyss of
    night?
    No climber dares to face the gulfs around ;
    Regards the rock-wall and the solid ground !
    And yet, as one who tastes the drowsy herb,

That doth imagination's flight perturb,
Craves ever more, so fierce desire to know
Burns fiercer, and contemns the vertigo. . . .
Then the cathedral bell began to toll;
And whelming waters boomed above my soul.

BOOK IV.

DISORDER.

BOOK IV.

DISORDER.

PROSE INTERLUDE. THE WORLD; OR, THE NEW WALPURGIS NIGHT.

THE WORLD IN THE CHURCH.

"AND now I caught a glimpse of one who, from his hyper-ecclesiastical deportment, preternatural gravity, and gaitered legs, I judged to be a bishop.   He, stiff, stately, and demure (with butler still more stiff, stately, and demure behind his chair), sat dining in a luxurious room of his episcopal palace, eating pheasant and sipping claret, while reflecting that his wine-merchants had certainly not supplied him with the same brand as before; next, that the rector of B——had not shown quite the full share of respect due to episcopal dignity, while latterly he had, from all accounts, shown a lamentable leaning towards the Sabellian heresy.   ['By the way, how very shabby his coat looked!   But the poor man has a parish of

10,000 souls, I believe, besides a wife and family—
I don't know how many—and about £50 a year to
keep them on! Jones'—to the butler—'just fetch
me Crockford!—this claret isn't Lafitte at all, Jones.'
(*Jones*—'Isn't it, my lord? Yes, my lord.') 'I'll
just see what the poor man has.'] Afterwards, his
lordship's thoughts reverted to the late imprudent
sale of a next presentation in which he was interested;
then to the dangerous encroachments of modern de-
mocracy in general, but of Nonconformity as regards
disestablishment and disendowment in particular;
lastly, to certain new-fangled, impracticable, and rather
indecorous notions put forward by some latitudinarian
brethren, concerning equalization of clerical incomes,
and curtailment of episcopal prerogative.

"The World in the Church! And ah! what profit-
less turning ever in the same closed circle of ideas!
What weariness in abstract thought! and mere pretentious emptiness in books! It's but the stone of
Sisyphus! I own that my high enterprise has suffered
defeat! Let me seek contact with life again; touch-
ing my native earth, I may renew my strength;
disillusioned, may become even reconciled to the
world. In any case, among men and women only
may theory be tested and verified. I may hear, too,
at first hand, what our latest thinkers and social reformers have to teach,—learn yonder what I could
not discover in solitude—some solution of modern

problems, some true panacea for the ills that afflict mankind.

"So from that hushed atmosphere of the Past, from those umbrageous elms and recumbent effigies of departed worth, from yonder oriel-windowed library of meditative seclusion, haunted silently by ardent thoughts of innumerable minds, thoughts that radiate from the printed page when one takes a volume, brown-bound, fragrant, fading, from amongst its fellows on the shelves, I found myself hurried once more to modern city and crowded street.—Over the mighty modern river, along whose banks roars Labour, myriad-armed, myriad-tongued; athwart whose vast bridges, traffic-thronged, thunders the lit train, whose cloudy breathing is fitfully illuminate; while under their huge arches, and betwixt their Titan piers, dividing the massy flood, swift, turbid, gurgling, corrugated, throb steamers laden with merchandise of all lands, and eager human faces—to the city of wharf, warehouse, dome, steeple, superb palace, and modern school, slum, hovel, court, alley, and street, loud with hubbub of wheels, glad song of children, call of itinerant vendor, drunken oath, filthy jest, maddened blow, shriek of pain!

The Palace of Art.

" In a wide and well-built thoroughfare of this
colossal city I noted how pompous Sir Capital
stalked majestic, save for occasional twinges of the
gout, or a tight boot ; but away from him I was trans-
ported to a chamber in a somewhat secluded square,
where I beheld Wordswords Schmetterling, an 'æsthete'
of prosperous and not ill-favoured countenance, composed to becoming melancholy, reclined at ease, in-
haling a perfumed narghileh, pastured upon sentiment,
ruminating airy fancies, and spinning his little cocoon
of versicles, wherein to hide himself from the vulgarity
and vexation of this everyday world. 'Religion,
philosophy, social questions, and politics are a
troubled element for art,' sighed this Göetheling, after
Göethe. And, accordingly, the poet had hung himself up (metaphorically speaking, of course) in the
quiet greenwood of a deserted London square, in-
habiting his little Paradise of dainty devices ; but
whether a seasonable change to winged activity would
ever happen to him, I knew not ; for look where, with
sinister smile, on the foot-pavement below, prowls a
too conscientious friend, and literary rival, seeking
whom he may devour in his next article, smacking
his lips over the prospect of how completely his pure
critical taste will constrain him to demolish his quon-

dam ally's little cocoon, and make a hearty meal of
the contents! But the pretty chrysalis, for the nonce,
remaining happily unconscious of this malign vicinity,
could achieve his delicate verbal effects in compara-
tive peace. These were really felicitous curiosities in
their way. And has not an indubitable poet justified
the grammarian for his life-long solicitude about ὅτε
and the enclitic δέ? At one's leisure these things
may help to kill time agreeably, and they show
dexterity. For me, I look, wonder, and pass.

"'Art,' said Schmetterling, talking to an acquaintance, who had now entered, 'has but to lisp nothings prettily, with a foreign accent, if possible, only
taking care that they be nothings. Let her, above
all, beware the pestilent heresy of supposing—though,
as you say, people like Æschylus, Sophocles, Shake-
speare, Lucretius, Dante, Milton, Shelley, Dryden,
Wordsworth, may have supposed—that Art has a
"mission"!—a mission to enlighten, fortify, or console.
Nay, if she forget to be a trifle, a plaything, she
ceases, *ipso facto*, to be Art.' 'Perhaps,' suggested
his acquaintance profanely, 'you and your school may
have a natural incapacity for, and therefore antipathy
to, serious thought, and this may explain your attitude.' 'On the contrary!' he replied. 'In fact, when
I was a boy, metaphysics were my favourite study.
But I went through, and exhausted all the philoso-
phies long ago, and found they had little to teach me

that I didn't know already—squeezed them dry—
mere pedantry, and empty phrases!' Here he took
a new pose, and blew a cloud of smoke. 'Besides,'
he added, 'the commonplace is alone capable of
wearing our precious adornments gracefully. In fact,
what we want is a lay figure to show off the pretty
dresses we make for it—the less animation the better.
And then there is nothing new to say! The world is
very old; all has been said; there is nothing very remarkable left for us to talk about now. One is dis-
enchanted—*blasé*, you know—*ennuyé*. Indeed, great
poets never really feel what they affect to feel—though,
of course, one must *simulate* feeling effectively. Now,
for instance, I have written some admired poems
about the sea. But I simply detest the sea! It
makes me ill even to go from Dover to Calais, you
know—what? Oh yes! my enemies say I have nothing but the gift of the musical gab, and am all
phrases. But, then, they are Philistines. Who is fool
enough to take a poet *au grand sérieux?* But to turn
a sentence or period cleverly is surely the highest of
human functions. Style, sir, style!—the one thing needful is style. No matter what you say, so long as you say
it nicely. It's rather a pity to have a big subject. That
is apt to be unwieldy. Doesn't it show more "genius"
to make one up for yourself, out of nothing at all—or
very little? However, if you can make a good thing
out of any subject, whatever it may be, in God's—

or the Devil's—name take it! A good thing, of course,
I mean, artistically speaking. What? Oh yes; pud-
ding and praise too will come by my method, plenty
of them! The slums, and the poor people! Oh, fie!
those can never be nice subjects, I should say! But
the nuances of subtle sentiment in refined persons and
artists—the delicate tint and tone, shine and shadow
of sensuous desire! only be sure to look at any
subject as a *subject*'—(' Providentially provided for you
to make poems out of,' added the friend)—'whether it
be the last earthquake, the plague, the story of a hero,
a royal marriage, or what not.' ('Just as cork-trees
were made to stop our ginger-beer bottles.') 'Art,'
resumed the poet, disdaining to notice this, 'is always
more than nature. What you have to do is to adorn
and polish her raw hard-grained rusticity.' 'Dear
me!' said the friend; 'I always fancied you poets
were lifted up by your subject, and penetrated by it,
carried out of yourselves, inevitably, as by a kind of
whirlwind, to lofty regions of artistic creation.' 'Oh,
that's quite exploded,' replied Schmetterling; 'just the
contrary! You must reduce the big subject to your
level—I mean, of course, elevate it to your level.'
('Patronize it, in short,' interrupted the other.) 'No,
but ours is the imaginative faculty, so much higher
than crude nature.' 'You must look at a thing
through the reverse end of your telescope, I suppose,
rather than use that to interpret it by,' put in the

Philistine. 'Well, then, it seems that the great events and tragedies of the world exist only in order to provide you fellows with the opportunity for illustrating the momentous distinction between Tweedledum and Tweedledee, trilled and quavered in dulcet numbers, as it were, by trained *ephebi* of ecclesiastical Rome. A great tragic event, a great public or private sorrow, is only so far important (in your eyes) as you may be able to tame or train it into a sort of circus horse, to show off its paces, and by caracoling display your skill and grace in equestrian feats of the literary *manége* before a gaping circle of intimates. In itself it is not of more or less moment than a mere passing whim or sensation of yourself, or of Jones, which may equally be elaborated into pyrotechnics of sensational and novel linguistic effect. You would "peep and botanize upon a mother's grave," nay, make a dead relation pose for you in becoming attitudes.' You leave out the morally beautiful and ugly, the intellectually satisfying, the higher proportion and loveliness pertaining to spirit, involving contrast between good and evil—that which is highest in man —only admitting the æsthetically or sensuously pleasing. With you, providing only you "rhyme and rattle, all is well." Poetry, according to your school, would seem to be the voluble, and more or less melodious gabble of a parrot, superadded to the posture-making and attitudinizing of a monkey,

or the airs and graces of a courtesan. But the art
has not been so understood by its great masters—
by Homer, Shakespeare, Schiller, Goethe, Hugo,
Byron, the Brownings, or Tennyson. Well, good-
bye.' 'What a Philistine,' muttered Schmetterling,
as he left. 'Knows as much of poetry and art as
my shoe!'

"It was said, I hardly know with how much truth,
that Schmetterling had deserted the wife whom (having one eye always pretty wide open on the main
chance) he had married, because, though she was an
excellent, domestic, affectionate soul, and devoted
mother, doing a great deal of good in the world, she
wasn't a '*genius*,' as he and his intimates fondly supposed themselves to be—that is, didn't sufficiently
appreciate the 'precious' verbal confections which
gave some people the idea of a very highly orna-
mented wedding-cake, and didn't care for the *feux
d'artifice*, or dodges of contorted diction. At any rate,
he gave himself the airs of a coxcomb with, and made
himself offensive to, many good, plain, straightforward
people, of far more essential and solid consequence
to mankind than himself, justifying his ignoble and
fretful selfishness on the implicit, if not avowed plea,
that such persons were not in his own private line of
linguistic confectionery and whipped syllabub, but
produced things less ethereal, or, as some horrid Philistines unkindly put it, 'more solid and nutritious, less

windy, salacious, and indigestible.' But can anything more utterly provincial, and ridiculous than such
an attitude be conceived? A true poet must first of
all be true man or woman. Imagine a Walter Scott
with all this deportment and affectation of a literary
Turveydrop, *petit maître*, or flunkey—Walter Scott, who
respected and made friends of so-called 'ordinary'
folk; of politicians, and those engaged in the various
professions; of workmen, tradesmen, dairymaids—
knowing that if they might learn something from him,
he, in his turn, had many things to learn from them, and
they their indispensable function, like himself.

> 'One bore his head above the rest,
> As if the world were dispossessed. . . .
> With measured step, and sorted smile . .
> Some trod out stealthily and slow,
> As if the sun would fall in snow
> If they walked to instead of fro.
> And some with conscious ambling free
> Did shake their bells right daintily,
> On hand and foot for harmony.'

So sang a great poet, and true woman, by the grace
of God born in the purple, and crowned, in scorn of
all pretenders.

"Then I, leaving this little Art-palace of the verbal
epicure, as finding less satisfaction here than in Church,
library, or temple of pleasure—no help for the solution

of problems that oppressed me, or consolation for world-sorrow—passed again into the street, noting on the pavement a work of ingenuity, made by a poor mechanic suffering from severe illness, that interested me almost more even than the felicitous curiosities within—though I did admire these, too, in their kind and in their degree. Only the manufacturers set such an inordinate value on their cobweb fabrics, their toys of musical wordmongery. This was a small wooden house, in which pith dolls were made to open windows and walk out of the doors when you dropped a penny into a slit made in the structure—really a very ingenious contrivance.

"Well, one mustn't break a butterfly upon a wheel, nor put one's stick into a wasps' nest! However, I wandered along the highway again, murmuring to myself with another great poet, 'Divine philosophy is not harsh and crabbed as dull fools suppose, But musical as is Apollo's lute.'

Good Society.

"Along an ample-mansioned street there approached now a well-appointed carriage with coachman and livery servant, in which were seated four persons of the first fashion—a man and woman of mature years, with two daughters, all fairly well-born, well-dressed, well-looking, negative people, not remarkable even for decorous indolence, that being so very common in their class. They wore an air of serene satisfaction with themselves and their belongings, tempered, however, by one of boredom, and relieved now and again by a look of half-ironical patronage, half-assumed unconsciousness, varied by a more pronounced and vulgarly insolent contempt in presence of those whom they were pleased to regard as their inferiors— persons, however, who often enough might be as verily superior to them as they were to the excremental dust under the hoofs of their horses; for while their embryos had evidently not been arrested at the tad- pole stage (through which, as we are told, all our embryos must inevitably pass) their souls had ap- parently remained behind somewhere about there, probably finding it too much trouble to go any further. These repose on the accomplished fact and established custom as comfortably as their bodies on the carriage cushions, since in their case the accomplished fact happens to turn uppermost for their convenience a general lounge quite as downy and luxurious, a soft agreeable surface of exceptional good fortune ; there, indeed, they repose, as though that were the very foundation of Kosmic order, unquestionably fit, proper, and eternally secure. Now, if this lounge should happen to have a seamy side turned down toward less favoured mortals underneath, and if these should have to make themselves as comfortable as possible under the circumstances in the obscurity of the nether parts—nay, should the human figures supporting the chair of state in which such persons pose prove no carven effigies in wood and stone, but a sort of living caryatides, rather—slaves, with the life-long contortion of limb and feature, the habitual corrugation of brow belonging to want, anxiety, and pain—as it were, perpetual bearers, sweating and agonized, on struggling shoulders, of emblazoned coffins containing so much dead weight of obstruction, royal, noble, or merely fox-facultied and moneyed,—why, such great folk do not often condescend to look so low ; and were their attention drawn to the circumstance, they might show plainly by their head-in-air deportment that they judged such an allusion indecorous and underbred in a modern drawing-room ; yet, should they prove equal to making a remark—which is improbable—it might be to this effect : that Providence having exclusive charge of all the arrangements, to question their propriety must be in singularly bad taste, not to say revolutionary and profane.   ' The poor ye have always with you,' quoted one of the ladies on some such occasion, listlessly buttoning the fourth button of her long kid glove.

" The existing order had the stolid support of these fine folk, partly because their minds were too sluggish readily to imagine any other, partly because the present system was entirely favourable to musty privilege.

They were orthodox and conservative in religious dogma also, so far as they were capable of comprehending it ; indeed, the less they understood, the more acquiescent were they ('We mustn't presume to question,' etc.)—if you put a dummy in a corner, it won't move ; it is a good Conservative, though rather deficient in private initiative.   This species of people, to adopt a phrase from the biology of polyps, has a *colonial*, rather than an individual consciousness—or, like Wordsworth's cloud, they 'move all together if they move at all.'   (That 'colonial' life is rather fine in its way, simulating and foreshadowing altruism at the opposite, inferior, and protoplasmic pole of the life cycle.)   Church and State, however, keep the people in their place, and it must be well to keep one's self in good odour with the higher Powers by paying them proper deference in the orthodox way—the only way which, one has always understood, has their special authorization and approval ; it must be as proper for us to touch our hats to them as for the lower classes to do it to us.

"The eldest daughter, now seated in this carriage, was about to marry a rich person of dubious reputation —with her eyes open ; the younger was affianced to an old 'hereditary legislator' of notoriously bad life —with her eyes shut.   And I thought to myself—After all, are these children better off than the murdered ones yonder, even than those who are sold by their poor parents to a life of shame, or kidnapped by mercenary wretches for purposes of prostitution?

"The carriage stopped before a large shop with expensive jewellery displayed behind plate-glass, and here the party alighted, being met and accompanied into the place by a young gentleman with an eye-glass, of similarly immaculate exterior and similarly inane cast of countenance—which, however, was not ill-adapted to assume a set stare of arrogant inquiry when any one out of his own set obtruded his presence or conversation. But there came to the carriage door a young woman of less immaculate exterior, the flush of strong drink, rouge, and consumption on her faded and haggard countenance, once beautiful, with a cough, and torn habiliments of tawdry finery, murmuring some hoarse request. She had once been a needle-woman; but making shirts at a penny a shirt is scarcely remunerative employment, while sitting stitching at them all day and half the night is a little trying to health; so that latterly she had preferred the streets. A policeman now told her to move on. One of the ladies, however, while proceeding from the carriage door to the shop under the shelter of the flunkey's big umbrella—for it was beginning to rain—ordered him to give her a penny, and passed in. .

RESPECTABILITY. "GETTING ON."

" Next in my dream it came to pass that all these distinguished persons seemed suddenly to be assembled together, and to recognize me. They all came up simultaneously—bishop, æsthetic reviewer, elderly peer (of juvenile creation)—and, with more effusion than I should have given them credit for, competed there and then for the pleasure of entertaining me. This made me regret the rather cynical point of view from which I had regarded them, and induced me to revise my verdict. I began to think I had done them some injustice, and to reflect that they were probably not bad fellows after all. I am not quite sure now whose invitation it was I accepted ; but I rather think it was the distinguished reviewer's (Mr. Worldlywiseman's), for I know I was consumedly anxious as to what he might say about my next book—yes, it was, for I remember that after disparaging the various nostrums advertised for human ills, he proceeded to advocate increased and more organized authority for journalism. He was a well-dressed man, with a somewhat supercilious air of serene superiority—an air of habitual minimizing, or depreciation—and an Oxford drawl. Like another sage, Socrates, he only knew that he knew nothing, but was evidently well contented with himself for knowing that much. His agnosticism appeared to agree with him; for he was sleek, gentle-manlike, and flourishing. As for his bitterness, that was his trade, and he had been a little sour from the cradle upwards. But he made it pay, and thanked the Unknowable that he was not as other men are—nor even as yonder poor ' dogmatist.'

" I found myself in a pillared hall of fine proportions, with wide balustraded staircase, then in a sumptuous dining-room, full of tables, about which waiters hurried, carrying many kinds of food. We dined—an excellent *menu* — and soon, in the luxurious, soft-carpeted smoking-room, I reclined in an arm-chair, sipping coffee, feeling that, after all, the actual order of things was not so very unsatisfactory—at least for me, who belonged to the privileged classes.

" What I really want (I avowed to myself in my present mood, and *sotto voce*) is to dominate, and know that I dominate; I want power, homage, and a great name. Social position is well, but by cultivation of natural gifts I will improve upon the advantage given by accident. Why not? The old name shall be illustrious; men shall bow down to me, and for this end I will adapt myself to their humours, study their predilections, gratify them by supplying what they happen to demand, trim my sails to the breath of popular applause, flattering the taste of the hour, powerful advocate of fashionable beliefs, or the shibbo-leths of some influential party. Much is to be said on every side, and I shall be half persuaded myself. My own ruling impulse shall be ridden with a curb; I will renounce, so far as may be, favourite studies, cherished ideals, if these are not likely to bring me speedy profit, praise, and an honoured name, being altogether outside the trend, sympathy, and comprehension of the common herd, cultivated or otherwise. Those wide gaping mouths of the many heads (which are mostly mouth) shall be supplied with the suitable pabulum. (What they may like or want at a given moment, indeed, may be almost as incalculable as the whims of a gust, that blows now one straw, and now another about the street!) Nor will I cherish my inmost private conviction, misgiving, or foreboding too conscientiously. Indeed, much must be sacrificed to party; great advances are only made by stern repression of idiosyncrasies and crotchets. Besides, some dirty work must be done; there must be some noise and friction of the machinery. One must live! Early ideals, like final causes, and vestal virgins, are apt to be barren. (Here the dissonant aerial chuckles became particularly harsh and loud.)

"These comfortable, though not too moral and original reflections, were meanwhile receiving reinforcement from the discourse of my host, which, though getting rather sleepy, I listened to with some edification and complacency—until, at least, he forgot the expediency, to use a slang phrase, of 'drawing it mild.' I can't recollect all he said, but amongst many wise things I recall these : He argued that philanthropy did more harm than good, because of its fanatical unwisdom. He showed incontrovertibly how much more mischief than benefit in the long-run well-meant remedies for popular grievances had invariably produced, since nature has so framed us that we *must* necessarily love ourselves and hate our neighbour. Philanthropists are merely meddling Pharisees, who set up to be better than their neighbours, and want to curtail individual liberty — an Englishman's house being his castle, etc. Are you going to pull down firmly-rooted abuses in a moment ? No, nor in a lifetime! They are tough, and take a deal of chopping. Don't fuss! What's the use? Besides, they are but symptoms of an ineradicable disease ; subdue them, and they will break out elsewhere, in some other shape. So my friend Worldly-wiseman observed, repressing a yawn, and an eructation—for we had both eaten a particularly good dinner —letting fall, at the same time, the long ash from his cigar, and ruminating his superfine article for next Saturday. In this style he now proceeded to expound 'the dismal science,' which may also, from another aspect of it, be named 'the comfortable creed,' till I thought he became rather dull, and only assented lazily, not half hearing, or caring to understand. I began to feel, indeed, that this kind of conventional acquiescence in the actual, however low and unrighteous, could hardly satisfy one long ; then, too, I was a Bohemian by nature, and that had a good deal to do with it ! Pleading the heat of the room, I went forth to breathe the air, and when I returned found, to my great relief, that mine host had gone to sleep. All through this conversation I had heard the low aerial voices chuckling. Quite as distinctly I heard them now as ever I had done in East-end slum, murderous country grange, or episcopal library ; then one whispered very audibly, as though to parody the really sensible remarks of my entertainer, 'Am I my brother's keeper ? '

"Was I a madman, or a 'medium,' a sort of magician, like my prototype, Dr. Faustus, who in the Middle Ages sold his soul to the devil for the sake of power, enjoyment, and occult, 'God-forbidden' lore—knowledge of what the spirit in man so ineradicably, if profanely, aspires to know? Certainly, I *seemed* to hold intercourse with spirits, good and bad, who spoke to me and influenced me for good and evil. But then the majority of scientists have pronounced that ' mediums ' are frauds and conjurers, when they are not victims of hallucination. And scientists surely must have exhausted all the evidence obtainable, both by personal investigation of these phenomena as they appear to occur in our own day, and by careful study of contemporary, as well as former testimony to their actuality. Yet, after all, is it possible that they have not paid sufficient attention to such things, since not a few very eminent men of science have pronounced the phenomena to be genuine? But far indeed be it from me to assert them genuine! for do not the majority of popular newspapers devote columns now and again to laughing at them? And the infallibility of newspapers, who would be presumptuous enough to question, even if one disbelieved in the Pope's? Why, they would review you unfavourably, or not at all! One would not even dare to whisper, 'E pur se muove!'—if it was a question of *tables*.

BABEL, AND WILL-O'-THE-WISP.

"Alas! I know too well that I shall be set down as a 'lunatic' anent these same 'voices'! There is no more certain note of 'lunacy' than hearing them, modern doctors tell us.

"A conversation going on in another part of the room had reference to kindred topics. Somebody was remarking how completely exploded for good and all is that old superstition about the inspiration of the Bible, or other sacred writings. He was demonstrating (by help of the marvellous illumination of modern science) how this kind of thing—namely, Bible-writing and miracles—is 'done:' it's partly honest

delusion of silly people, and partly pious fraud, clever
conjuring which has managed to impose itself on
gaping ignorance, or barbaric simplicity as supernatural.   For we now so perfectly comprehend *all* the
laws of nature, and know so certainly that all must
happen through one or other of the laws with which
we are already familiar !   And perhaps wisdom will
die with us.   For do not there seem (if that indeed be
possible in so enlightened an age !) to be some ugly
symptoms of a recrudescence of superstition in the
shape of table-turning and spiritism?   But ours, alas !
may be only a thin slice of sound, substantial scep-
ticism, nutritive and consoling, sandwiched in between
two huge interminable hunches of windy, unwholesome
superstition, euphoniously christened ' Faith.'   Ah !
those long dark ages, that have only just ceased for
our poor humanity, and may yet recommence !—why,
there was that poor old Pagan fool, Socrates—almost
as bad as a Christian !—with his ' demon,' and his
maundering chatter about ' the Good,' ' the Beautiful,' ' the True,' and the immortality of the soul !
The mere mention in his hearing of the ' Demon,' and
the ' Voices,' would have been enough to show our
great Dr. M—— what was the matter with *him*—how
seriously the cortical tracts—the grey matter, or the
white (these are the only true ' white spirits and grey '
of the old song !)—had gone astray in the upper storey
of that ugly, prophetic skull !   And then the poor old

fellow need only have been clapped into a comfortable asylum (conducted on the benevolent modern system) —need not have been requested to swallow that poison ! But ah ! great Dr. M—— was yet unborn, nor was anything then known about the *hippocampus minor;* such knowledge being reserved for our own favoured times (that 'they without us should not be made perfect,' I suppose)—for this illuminated age of universal and exhaustive knowledge—(tempered, indeed, it occurred to me, by simultaneous professions of general ignorance, and supreme despair !)   Seers, prophets, and reformers, forsooth ! At last we have found out what to do with *them !* Send them to some celebrated mad-doctor; on no account stone, or burn them ! That's but a crude way of hurting, and getting rid of them, with their disagreeable ways.   It isn't their 'cussedness,' as the world once supposed ; it's only their hippocampus a little out of order ! Put them in a strait-waistcoat, and take no more notice ! Let 'the wind blow where it listeth !' For we have found out that it is *only* wind ; therefore let us be joyful !— 'the spirit does but mean the breath.'   After all, one reflected, this is only a learned and more scientific adoption and adaptation of the vulgar herd's normal and natural attitude in presence of genius, its heaven-accredited ruler and guide—a more elaborate and instructed way of kicking against the pricks.   Cassandra, what sayest thou ? Paul, what did a certain

Festus think of thee? And what, at a later date
was the doom of Tasso? But in those days they
supposed that

> 'The dog, to gain his private ends,
> Went mad, and bit the man;'

and so he got uncommonly short shrift. Though
whether 'Crucify, crucify!' or 'Shut him up as a
lunatic!' be the more agreeable cry to hear, we may
leave to the prophet whom we are hounding to
determine. However, whether, again, these, or the
multitude that bellows after them, thirsting for blood,
be the more insane, some of us may feel disposed to
apply here with modification the words, 'Heu!
quanto minus reliquis versari quam tui meminisse!'
And it must be admitted that these insane folk have
given the world a few powerful onward shoves, in
spite, if not on account, of their insanity! Unless,
indeed, it was only some strangely inexplicable thought-
dominating spell, cast upon mankind everywhere and
always by a crafty (though rather dull and stupid)
priesthood, who, in their own interests, got them to
believe those obvious fables about God, human personality, and an after-life for retribution or compen-
sation, equitable conclusion, and explication of the
inequalities in earthly lots. Absurd and immoral
ideas, which, left to their own unsophisticated reason
and conscience, men would so unhesitatingly have

rejected ! Strange, almost miraculous influence of a
by no means exceptionally gifted, but very average
class of persons all over the world ! But the present
life has lately been discovered to be so eminently
satisfactory to all concerned—especially to the majority
of poor toilers, clothed in hodden grey, besmirched
with grime of want and vice, blood and tears, whose
children call to them day and night for food which
they cannot provide, till over and over again they resolve
to end it all for themselves and those dear to them by
friendly knife or poison—that it is manifestly puerile
and superfluous to concern one's self about any other.
And if there be still something wanting to our earthly
paradise, can we not secure the millennium to-
morrow by incontinently dividing the accumulated
earnings of a clever and industrious few among the
idle and incompetent many, so that all may have a
very little, if not quite enough? Is it obvious, indeed, that, natural abilities and moral virtues not
being so easily divisible, the result and outcome of
this forcible, and eminently righteous distribution will
not be the same inequality to-morrow morning? But,
of course, we must grease our new social machine
with a little human fat, so as to make it move more
easily, painting it gaily also with a little gore. We
shall have to slit a few gullets. But blood-letting in
the civil organism is a healthy process of depletion,
which you can notoriously arrest just at the precise

amount and period your own judicious and humane fancy may happen to suggest. It's as simple as putting warm water into a bath ; you have only to turn your private tap, and the red stream ceases flowing. The temperature of social strife, moreover, for all the world like that of a warm bath, can so easily be regulated by your own little thermometer. Past experience proves it, blood feuds and wars of revenge being unheard of in Europe, or elsewhere.

" 'An eye for an eye, and a tooth for a tooth' is doubtless an exploded principle, only known to the ancient Jews. Those age-long degradations of insolent contumely, repression, neglect, and inhuman persecution that characterized feudal Europe were doubtless as little responsible for the frenzied orgy of cruel and general murder that marked the first French Revolution, as were the massacre of priests and hostages and the burning of their own fair city by the Paris Commune for those retaliatory excesses of the White Terror. Nay, but the ineffable horde of barbarous roughs, tricoteuses, and petroleuses, which our so-called ' civilization' considerately nurses in the Pandemonium of her huge cities, and disembogues on festive or anti-festive occasions, are precisely what our ever-enduring criminal and callous stupidity has carefully contrived and provided for world-confusion. And will they not destroy us, as those outer barbarians destroyed Rome ?

"Ah! no—slowly and tentatively, founding themselves on experience, patiently, with mutual sympathy,
justice, kindness, let our fresh-leafing institutions grow
in the free illuminated air of wise and virtuous conviction, branching and burgeoning out of the old
primal root of Divine and Human Veneration, out of
the ancient order, until there rise, in the course of
ages, as to a hidden music, nobly proportioned, the
City of God!

"Thus spake one dissenting from the glib and
sinister, though plausible, panaceas so airily pro-
pounded, and continued—

"Alas! though men inherit the vices, how seldom
do they profit by the experience of their forefathers!
One would think, to hear some talk, that we were all
back early in the last century, in full Floréal, offering
votive flowers of our fraternity upon the ancient altars,
and fervently embracing one another, when Hope was
yet young, and the weary peoples were turning eager
eyes toward that daydawn of Liberty, so soon, alas!
to be extinguished, lurid and cloud-mantled, setting
in seas of blood ; one would suppose that the frown-
ing Bastilles of hoar Tyranny had but now fallen amid
the glad triumphant pæans of emancipated Humanity
—ere Revolution, agape for more victims, like any
Tiberius, or Commodus, like any De Sade, De Retz,
or Catherine de Medici of the old *régime*—after
spawning Marat, Hebert, Fouquier-Tinville, and the

'Seagreen Incorruptible,' born with hands clutching
one another's throats, mad with mutual hatred, suspicion, and envy—had devoured her own evil brood,
and organized civil society, reverting to primal chaos,
the ever-unfortunate People, hoodwinked as usual,
betrayed by knaves and fools, uncrowned and un-
decorated this time, starved again as heretofore—until
the inevitable Despot arose to stamp with mailed heel
upon the Hydra, chaos-clamouring, blood-gorged. No!
bloodshed, revolution, and violent overturning are but
a poor remedy—save in countries where no constitu-
tional, no public cry can make itself heard in the
general night, but all is stifled by the moral murderer.
Yet blandly or sullenly do sanguinary fanatics, cynical,
self-seeking, untaught and unteachable, propose to us,
of the later Nineteenth Century, the same old seesaw
of civil fury and mutual slaughter, as supreme panacea
for all wrong, supreme satisfaction for all want! What!
Have we of later time never gazed, then, into the pit
of massacre at Avignon, in that accursed Palace of
Popes, with 'citizens' who made their brutal jest
upon the lingering agonies of men, women, and
children, writhing and moaning there, a confused dim
heap in the horrible darkness? never seen the
drunken Septemberers hacking blunderingly at de-
fenceless victims, whetting their newly acquired,
unnatural appetite for blood and torture in those
paven courts and dungeons of Paris Prison? never

heard the sinister roll of tumbrils, laden with their matutinal human food for Death? beheld refined and gentle women, friends of man, insulted and torn to pieces by a 'fraternal' mob of 'sisters,' 'brothers'? or an amiable child done to death by them, only because he happened to be born royal? Ah! sweet and lovable human nature! As Byron says—

'Religion, virtue, freedom, what you will,
A word's enough to rouse mankind to kill!'

"The note of this new panacea for all our woe seems to be—Eliminate the head for the benefit of the hands; let the former perish of atrophy, that the latter may be well nourished. It is an old-fashioned notion that the head is wanted to cater for the hands. This was concisely put by a sansculotte Caliban at a public meeting recently, when he howled, 'After all, Shake-speare was a b——y blood-sucker, for *he* never made so much as a pair of shoes!' Perhaps under the new *régime* technical and industrial schools may still be permitted; but probably there will be little place or leisure for such mere luxuries as learning or art, for their own sakes. Genius will be formally declared (what it virtually is now) a penal offence, because it testifies to inequality, and the ideal is a dead level of Philistine mediocrity, in which the barren plain may have the satisfaction of feeling itself equal to the

H

fruitful hill, which it can hardly do till the latter has been properly pared down. Man must revert to pure stomach and claw, partly because he is all body, though he affects to be also spirit; and to vegetate in bodily comfort ought to be his chief concern, partly that his own flesh and blood, which he is pleased to stigmatize as 'lower animals,' may no longer feel offended by his superiority. Those aboriginal gorillas, when the first simian aristocrat showed signs of incipient evolution, ought obviously to have pro-tested, and nipped that bloated man-monkey in the bud. The golden age sung by poets will surely arrive when all shall have been reduced to the low standard of our own pet average inferiority—for, as it is our own, must it not be best?—when no discovery and no invention, no original work in art, no heroic exemplar of illustrious life shall any longer be possible. Neither may there be any more spontaneous sacrifice of right, or pleasure for alien good; forbidden shall be free play of limb, and gracious colour of distinctive indi-viduality in joyous self-development; all shall be one monotony of cast-iron under the stupid tyranny of a jealous multitude, incapable of sympathetic admiration for what is different from themselves, though equally natural and needed, incapable of reverence for what is above, exalting into an idol *Custom*, which is the dense folly, the base and stunted unloveliness of each one multiplied into that of all his neighbours. None of us have any superiors ; that notion is a relic of servility and dependence. The way to succeed in a given undertaking is to quench the adepts and past masters in it, so as not to risk offending any infusorial or Lilliputian susceptibility, that its possessor may be able to hold up the little head, and strut with conceit unruffled, complacently boasting its own ability in full measure to 'whip creation.' For has not the ostrich taught us to ignore unwelcome facts by hiding our heads in the sand ? If a grand guide, born upon the flank of a mighty mountain, offered to show some puny, black-coated citizen from yonder plain the direct and easiest way up to the summit, at all hazards let the free and enlightened cockney insist that his guide shall go behind, or abreast, and on no account in front of him ! Oh ! that will be joyful, when all is marsh and croaking frog, when the mountain shall be level with the morass, and there shall be no eagle to soar over it, or invite to aspire heavenward ! What a sweet place the world would be if we could only rid ourselves of Miranda and Ferdinand by a process of throat-cutting, and so prevent any further propagation of their insolent superiority, for then should we be left free to populate it *ad libitum* with Caliban and Sycorax, made in our own ugly image. Then what comfortable sprawling and wallowing in muck-heaps, well beloved ! with no remonstrance, or reprehension more from any possible censor ! Then would the world revert to that halcyon epoch, unfortunately left so far behind, when those dear 'dragons of the prime, tare one another in their slime.'

("The running comment on suchlike astounding proposals for ameliorating the lot of man, by suppression of all his aspirations after a veritable amelioration —even now, I should have imagined, too rare for the much to be desiderated evolution of higher possibilities in him—may, indeed, be mine, but the substance of them is correctly reported, and they certainly appeared to me infatuated beyond measure.)

"If a source be poisoned, then (said another interlocutor, differing) all you have to do is to alter the arrangement of the conduits ; that will make the water drinkable and wholesome ; 'cœlum, non animam mutant, qui trans mare currunt.' Ah ! but that man was a fool, for he talked Latin, and not English ! At any rate, *we* know that the regeneration of a man's soul is secure if only he can remove into a larger and better furnished house over the way. Taylor's vans, in the light of this discovery, acquire a quite sacred, novel, and mystic significance. Man never wants more than the golden mean, which is a fixed quantity, the exact area of which any common measuring tape is, of course, competent to determine. You only need add to this virtue of external prosperity a little blue pill, or a liver pad, in case of internal derangement, and then the human subject will be 'thoroughly furnished unto all good works.' 'How hardly shall the rich man,' was a slip of the tongue; congratulation, rather, having been intended. Only that the *wrong* people are rich now; and fairly may *they* be denounced. Let riches change hands, and all will be right for ever. Or are there no bad and unhappy rich men? I thought there were, and that this was what the row was all about.

"Yet when another speaker alluded to the main social problem at present being a right distribution of our great wealth among the people at large, he spoke wisely. Think of the shame and horror of workhouse, or starvation, as only alternative goals possible on our present economical system to a long career of honest toil; think of the terrific chasms that sever classes, the unequal proportion of wage, or profit paid to manual labour. A *minimum* of material property and well-being is the *Pou sto* and fulcrum for spiritual or intellectual progress. What of our white slave-girls, slaving night and day for a pittance insufficient to keep body and soul together, till their very flesh and blood compels them to sell their souls to the devil, whether they will or no? Think of our national prosperity, our luxury, our comfort, our domestic respectability, and the sweet, happy, cleanly virtue of our sisters and daughters, all founded complacently upon this quicksand of hideous wrong, that

cries to all the worlds and all the abysses for redress
—cries night and day, till One descend to avenge
—set in order this world-confusion—to avenge the
souls of them crying under the altar. And shall
He not avenge His own elect, although He tarry
long? or shall this quaking quicksand unaware
engulf all? Every man, woman, and child has a
sacred, inviolable, inalienable individuality, that may
claim as a right from society respect, sympathy, and
free development. While the separation and want
of familiar intercourse between classes, together with
the excessive division of labour, are very deeply
to be deplored. All honest and useful work demands appreciation, with equitable remuneration. It
is not equality of material prosperity that we want—
nor worship and slavish prostration before wealth, as
an idol—nor, indeed, before any other social, racial,
or mental distinction; though honour be due to it, if a
real one. Refinement, race, talent, beauty, are worthy
of all honour; but so, also, are goodness, and honest
work. Thus said the speaker, and one assented with
all the heart. Let men or women (he continued) seek
for *congenial* occupation, if that can be found; but,
above all, let them respect themselves, and claim
respect from others as honourable producers for the
family and the community, whatever their function,
not feverishly aspire to change their sphere for
one more conventionally, but not more veritably,

estimable, in hope to win a false and hollow consideration from fools, a cordial welcome into the charmed circle of inane automata, all varnish and all veneer.

"He talked admirable sense about the expediency of co-operative production, and the obligation on all, as members of a community, to contribute their share of labour for the common good. Socialism, while exaggerated and short-sighted, points out the *direction* of our future progress, though not precisely the right road. There is, indeed, a minimum of material well-being, without which no spiritual life, as a rule, is possible. 'Give me neither poverty nor riches.' But different kinds of work are needed, and a leisured class seems also needed to secure that fit and right variety; while no complete development, or absolutely equal partition of this world's goods is possible for all, here and now; nor, were it possible, would it be very desirable. Patience and faith are always needed, and by every man, in view of our frailty, and the incalculable dealings with us of human destiny. While as for idleness, there is a fertile and wise idleness. It is a good thing to know how and when to loaf. The stupid tyranny of a Philistine majority is bad enough in its unwritten code of 'public opinion,' blown about by tea-table tittle-tattle; what would it be consolidated into parchments, and driven home by vigilance committees,

or prying inspectors? Individuality, within social
limits broad and tolerant, needs nurture and protec-
tion ; yet to do work of public benefit more effectually,
doubtless the State may profitably and equitably inter-
vene—also to nurture and protect the weak.

But what shall be said of the anarchist proposal
to have women, as well as property, in common?
The latter proposal violates the sanctities of privacy
and liberty ; but the former deserves rather a cat-o'-
nine-tails than a reply. Woman, after generations
beginning to win her own from brute force, to be
delivered over again for toy, chattel, and random
rut of the human boar? Had these Calibans, then,
no mothers? Did their fathers copulate with sows
in some stye, or sprang they from chance semen spilt
there by the Evil One, and fertile after the fashion
of dragons' teeth in ancient story? Or were their
mothers *succubæ*, pregnant perchance from some rape
of *incubi*, ascended from the lowest pit?

"But, indeed, we are to begin *de novo*, reverse the
growth of heredity and evolution, make a *tabula rasa*
of the past by act of parliament, jump off our own
shadows, retrospectively quash and cancel the mother's
milk that nourished us, post up at the town hall
a bye-law for the abolition of the air we breathe, and
let a vestry quorum vote the elimination of all the
blood from our bodies, as tainted ancestrally, open to
grave suspicion of political obscurantism, as deriving

from a feudal origin.   Or—no—let's have a *plébiscite !*
That, as a 'cute popular journal assured us lately,
is sure to be infallible—Obviously! For was it not
a *plébiscite* which chose Barabbas, and rejected Christ ;.
in politics, embraced the second French empire; in
literature, preferred Waller and Cowley to Milton ;
Samuel Rogers, and Tom Moore (true, yet inferior
poets) to Landor, Shelley, Keats, Wordsworth, and
Coleridge ? Therefore, sirs, let us have your ' voices !'

" Meanwhile, one would suppose that (whatever may
be in store for them of earthly prosperity, over and
above that spirit of greed, envy, class-hatred, and
blood-thirstiness, inculcated by their prophets as
promising dispositions for securing happiness) the
majority hitherto have hardly enjoyed such a surfeit
and superfluity of good things here that their gorge
need rise at the very mention of a fuller and more
invigorating meal provided elsewhere ! Are they the
persons, then, whose stomachs have been so crammed
that they insist upon a plethoric slumber of indiges-
tion, which must not on any account know waking—
having done work, moreover, of such transcendent
value for the universe that they desire henceforward
to be put on the retired list, and pensioned off in
perpetuity, while the world moves on its high and
majestic course, with no help more, or shadow of
passing interest from them ? Ought not the universe
to be grateful for what it has got from them already,

leaving them henceforward to rest in peace, rousing
them no more from slumber, early or late, but suffering them to rot indolently in graves, while the
Triumph of Life passes onward, while the wonderful
Yggdrasil of Ages burgeons ever, and ripens in fruit
and flower—in fruit and flower of suns and satellites,
with their teeming infinitude of mutually-involved,
and included conscious lives? But the eternal alms-
house *they* would retire to, with idleness for everlasting dole, is Annihilation. 'No, we won't play
any more !—the nature of things in general has dis-
gusted us too thoroughly.' Surely this is but a
spurious altruism, that overleaps itself, and falls on
the other side ! So nobly oblivious of self are they,
so absorbed in active and contemplative sympathy
with the universe, that they become perfectly contented such disinterested sympathy should cease,
relapsing into everlasting indifference, after an hour !
Is not that a lop-sided, topsy-turvy altruism, that does
not really know what it wants, or why, but proceeds
to contradict, devour, and defeat itself? And do
they show unselfishness quite up to such high
standard in their present lives? Self-sacrifice, self-
absorption, if you please !—but that is possible only
on condition that there remain, though implicit, a
self to be 'sacrificed,' or 'absorbed' ! So much for
the *ethical* aspect—

   " And as for the *intellectual ;* if the sole conceivable,

discriminating, comparing, remembering organizer and constitutive element of any possible experience, one self-identifying, conscious individuality, one and self-identical through all change, be not the permanent, substantial factor of existence, above birth and death, beyond time and space, what is it?

"Being, Force, the Unknowable, the Unconscious —these are mere thin abstractions from the living real Human, with its intellect and emotion; all phenomena are necessarily phenomena of some consciousness, which is the only integrating, differentiating Power we can conceive possible; while all consciousness is necessarily individual, however superior to our actual imperfect consciousness—however all-embracing by sympathy, transcending by inclusion —necessarily involves emotion also; otherwise, where do we obtain it?—So I heard an interlocutor say. Well, at all events (he proceeded), do not let these sulky dyspeptics of the school of Schopenhauer pose as martyrs and heroes, sublime in self-abnegation! *That* is a little too much. It's all their modesty—who are they that they should live again? '*Wollt ihr immer leben?*' as Mr. Carlyle's hero said to his 'food for powder.' Of what further use can they presume to be? Well, if they feel themselves played out, and surfeited with success or notoriety, perhaps the universe *may* graciously dispense with their future services, and send them about their business into that

oblivious and oblivioned nonentity, which they modestly
judge most suitable to their humble requirements;
and, after all, who should know better than themselves
about that? Possibly wind-bags, after pricking, are
with difficulty blown out again. I admit that if I
were freely mentioned by my friends, and quoted in
the cheap press, little would remain to me but to sing
the *Nunc Dimittis*, and shut up for ever after. Of
this, alas! I have no experience; but it must needs
be a soul-satiating one, assuredly. Indeed, if I had
thus been voted among 'the immortals,' so sure
should I be of my 'immortality,' that, in order to
secure it, bedad, wouldn't I (my friend was evidently
an Irishman, and perhaps the grapes were sour!) per-
form the 'happy despatch' forthwith, upon myself
and upon them, lest one day I should cease to deserve
their favours, or my immortalizers should change
their minds, and so deprive me of a little decoration,
obviously in the power of a few casual passers-by to
confer, (too evidently the speaker was envious of those
on whom the decoration *had been* already conferred—
by themselves and their disciples—and who had thus
become already indisputably 'immortal!')—posterity
notoriously holding itself bound to confirm all the
transitory whims of its forefathers, however self-con-
tradictory! And an immortality in human gabble, so
long as a language lasts, and no Caliph Omar burns a
library—what an honour! Ah, me! how many fine

things destined for immortality have long since rotted upon the dust-heap, been diverted from their high destiny to glut the maw of Oblivion. 'C'est Boulanger qu'il nous faut!' And some one else to-morrow —Napoleon yesterday. Proud Sesostris, indeed, before whom the world trembled, grand and awful even in death, sealed 'for ever' in his royal pyramid, to-day is fingered, and his identity disputed, by black-coated professors of alien race—a race then all undreamed in the womb of a far future—at Boulaq, or British Museum; next he may furnish an object-lesson for one of our Board-schools, to illustrate the ancient art of embalming mummies! And, ah! how many 'immortal' bards of ancient Egypt are very dead indeed; or let somebody now call over but their names? 'Unknown, and unknowable!'

"Inspiration of bibles, and revelations, forsooth (I heard one of the clever men in this group say)! We are rather too wide-awake for that now. Why, we can give you an infallible receipt for writing bibles— tell you all the ingredients—only be sure to mix them well, and put in the right proportions! At all events, we can furnish you with a neat algebraical formula, which shall adequately represent their composition by symbolizing our exhaustive analysis of the process. Here it is—A, B, C, D—very simple and easy to remember. Let A stand for the right hemisphere, or *dextro*-cerebral, ideational nervous centres of the brain,

B for the word-hearing, C for the image-seeing, D for the word-writing centres. Then this right hemisphere being nothing but a man-trap, a sheer delusion-mongering department, in that pulpy thought-manufacturing apparatus so obligingly provided for man by the step-motherly solicitude of that great 'Unknowable,' in whose charge he finds himself, it is evident that when this interferes, its influence (if a play upon words may be permitted) must prove quite dexterously sinister; and the person will find himself most unmercifully hoaxed, and hocussed merely by the malign interior arrangements of his own nature and constitution. For the brain is discovered to be a material mill, ingeniously adapted for grinding grist that has never been brought to it—cornflour out of stones—consciousness, namely, out of the Unconscious—reason, love, moral judgment, and sensibility out of oxygen, nitrogen, and carbon, arranged in the form of albumen. All the secret lies in the arrangement. Shuffle the elements well! And then, hocus pocus! The conjurer's hat is nothing to it. 'Walk up, walk up, ladies and gentlemen! See Christmas Day put into my hat! and Westminster Bridge emerge!' That makes all so simple, doesn't it? Now, the *sinistro*-cerebral department of this potent automatic god-and-man manufactory is capable of turning out a much more decent and reliable article in the way of gods and men than the *dextro*-cerebral.

" 'Who, then, or what constructed this patent god-and-man manufactory itself, if *it* is the origin of ourselves, and of all we know?' I ventured to put in here. But I got as little of a satisfactory answer as Alice got from the Mad Hatter. Indeed, that tea-party she went to appeared to me very similar, on the whole, to this club-gathering of 'men of light and leading.' However, *I* seemed to be a sort of inaudible and invisible ghost to these good people, who apparently were unaware that any one out of their own circle had spoken. This, indeed, was a dream, and queer things happen in dreams. But has not many a waking poet experienced the same feeling before? I am informed that it is rather like trying to breathe in an exhausted receiver, or fly easily about in a vacuum. I felt sorry I spoke, though something, I suppose, will make me speak again. People, it is true, have a way of not hearing disagreeable or puzzling questions. Perhaps they don't always understand them.

" The *dextro*-cerebral department (he proceeded gravely, and with conviction) is, indeed, responsible for all this fatuous mischief of bible-making, ecclesiastical authority, superstition, and so on. Nay, it actually has the impudence to set up for a second (though unconscious) individuality inside our own, simulating some foreign intelligence and character apart from and opposed to ours—while actually part and parcel of ourselves all the time ! Thus are we all born with a treacherous imp established in the very citadel of our own personality. And, worse luck! we cannot turn him out—a parasite nourished upon our own life-juices! Well, see now how reprehensible is the conduct of this masquerading, secondary self, pretending to be some one else—this ill-conditioned Puck of a right hemisphere, whom we have called A ! What does it now do ? Why, it proceeds to play upon B, the word-hearing, and C, the image-seeing nervous centres—without any provocation whatsoever, or injunction from outside, from any real object—but just out of sheer native love of mischief, and disposition to practical joking, however tremendous the consequences upon its unfortunate conscious companion, condemned to live with it in the same skull. For this of course makes the man to whom it happens suppose that he hears a message of transcendent import from some angel, or, perhaps, even from god himself (it is better to write this name with a small *g*, and so discourage superstition), which he is commissioned to deliver to the world. Then at once D, the word-writing centre, is, by means of a diabolically ingenious piece of mechanism (verily, a sort of physiological infernal machine !) set to work, and writes the message down—becomes, in fact, the property and servant for the time being of this concealed conspirator; just as if foreigners in the guise of natives should possess themselves of a telegraph office, and send false news to the national government. So do bibles, and illusory revelations get themselves scribbled off by the yard, to the profit of priests, and such-like blood-sucking leeches of the community! It is too shameful!

"But in the present day we are without excuse if we remain ignorant of these things. Are we masters in Israel, and know them not? For all that is needed is some elementary information about physiology, which, with our Board-schools and cheap primers, is easily attainable. Fancy these messages claiming to be Heaven-descended, while as a matter of fact descending from no higher or sublimer source than the disordered right hemisphere of a fool's skull, setting up for itself, ventriloquizing and masquerading for its own amusement! It may be rather odd that thought *should* rise so much higher than its own level; but that old law about levels applied only to water, and, moreover, being so old, it is very probably repealed by this time; or if not, why, it ought to be! And this is the kind of thing that was for so long, and so universally, supposed to be given by Divine inspiration, as also to be 'profitable for reproof, for correction, and for instruction in righteousness!' To think that a little ordinary cram on the part of any elementary examination-coach of the present day would have sufficed to set right

these stupendous mistakes of old wiseacres imagined
to be prophets of the human race, had it been heretofore attainable—would have correctly informed the
world's apostles, preventing altogether, for instance, the
propagation of Christianity, Buddhism, and other absurd
religions, by us in these latter days finally exploded !

"These mistakes, moreover, have been, singularly
enough, committed not only by savage races, by poor
and ignorant people, but by the highest intellects, the
most transcendently virtuous and heroic natures, rest-
ing, all of them, small and great, weak and powerful,
on those same fictitious promises, and hollow conso-
lations, which—while they proved mighty to the pulling
down of strongholds—endowed men, women, and
children also with patient strength to bear and conquer
fate, confront with serene resolve extremest rigour of
suffering, unintermittent blows of hard misfortune,
welcome the last enemy with a smile of triumphant
joy, in ' sure and certain hope '—yet all had for sole
origin some diseased pulp within the cranium, aided
by the calculating machinations of a doting priest !
Verily this same cellular pulp is a potent magician,
responsible for a good deal. Hudibras informs us that—

> ' Bombastes kept a devil bird,
> Shut in the pommel of his sword.'

But what was that familiar spirit to these so potent
and perverse dextro-cerebral centres we all keep

shut in our own skulls? But, then, has not the old
poet shrewdly noted from what insignificant causes
greatest events are wont to spring? 'This is the
victory that overcometh the world, even your faith.'
Ah! how much better, then, to be overcome by the
world, and trampled under its iron feet, or go down in
some fierce strife, endeavouring with unprofitable fury,
born of envy and unreason, to wrest from it that uniform
success, that external prosperity, which eternal laws
deny, which would be so disappointing when obtained,
and which, passionately sought, only fires with inextinguishable craving for more and more. Why, it
is the very fuel which feeds hell-flame, they are
bidding us seek, desiderate, or steal! At all costs let
us remain undeluded, now that an infallible *physical*
science has, once for all, authoritatively belittled and
bemocked for us the *spiritual* hopes and heritage of a
heretofore bamboozled humanity! 'Conscience and
affection demand satisfaction as much as sense and
understanding,'—did you say?—'and are as much
entitled to receive it. That cannot be true, which
flouts and insults them.' Nay, you rave! What
are these? Can you see or touch them? Are they
something good to eat? Do they bring power,
comfort, consideration? Sense, and the pigeon-
holing faculty called understanding are the only
possible and legitimate organs of knowledge. At any
rate, they have *our* authorized and official imprima-

tur, while your spiritual aspirations and intuitions are consigned to our *index expurgatorius.*

"This discussion was going on not far off, between the illustrious Professor Bathybius, and some one who seemed to disagree with him, stemming with difficulty the strong flood-tide of materialism and negation. These, then, are specimens, I thought, of the mental and moral husks, or thistles, which some folk are content to eat, and this is what we are offered in place of the 'everlasting gospel!' That has been overlaid, too well I know, with man's perversity, misunderstanding, and corruption; but at least there is a kernel of nourishing food there, a gleam from thence upon the outer darkness; here, none at all, only confusion worse confounded, a fatuous, self-complacent rejection of all reason and all hope. Were Ezekiel, John of Patmos, and all the old seers, then, born naturals? And Milton? And he who saw the visions of hell, heaven, and purgatory, singing, 'In la sua voluntade e nostra pace'? And a Greater than these, who imagined that He came from God, and went to God, His inmost spirit remaining in heaven even while He was upon earth, revealing God to men? Oh! the great assurance of the little blind guides, glorying in their blindness, who dare fancy it!

"Yet to none do I yield in admiration for, and gratitude to Science herself, that latest and best teller of fairy-tales, when she discovers new uses, wonders, and beauties in the outer world of nature, as in our own bodies; only let her stick to her own last, nor intrude into regions too high for her, with her pseudo-explanations, and arrogant denials, questioning the competency of her elder sisters, Theology, and Metaphysique, in those provinces, which were native to them of old before she was born. 'For,' said the idealist, addressing Professor Bathybius, 'if the cerebral process, even with the intervention of an object admittedly external to the individual perceiver (whether real or ideal is not now the question), cannot at all explain the normal perception of colour, form, solidity, and so on, or the veriest elementary sensation—which is the fact—how is it going to explain that more uncommon intuition of a super-sensible sphere, and the sublime relations appertaining thereto, without the intervention of any corresponding super-sensible object? If all be subjective hallucination in the last case, why not also in the former? which yet common sense pronounces an absurd conclusion. For then there could be no intercourse of man with man, no justification for the belief that any person exists other than one's own particular self. Nor is it any answer to appeal to a common consent present in one case, but absent in the other, because, first, the objectivity of other persons has to be *assumed* before any argument can be founded upon their consent;

and, secondly, the conditions of normal perception
are probably alike for ordinary perceivers, whereas
they are evidently different for the extraordinary,
which would quite sufficiently account for the latter's
perception and comprehension being different also,
without supposing illusion in one case, and not in the
other. Above all, how can the brain be the source,
and cause of thought and sensibility, to say nothing of
conscience and affection, when the very notion of a
brain itself involves a pre-formed, pre-existing thought
and sensibility, to make this very brain conceivable at all ? Brain and body are notions of some
thinker, implying the conscious unity, and implicit
self-identification of that thinker in memory, as also
his comparing, distinguishing faculty.' * I confess I
thought the idealist had the best of it here. The
Professor, however, in reply, made his little joke.
He said, 'Don't be too hard on brains ; leave that to
the clergy ; they are interested in depreciating brains,
and so may stand excused ! Besides, what you say is
mysticism. It means nothing—at least, it's too deep
for me. I don't understand you.' And the popular
press agreed with him. Yet to grin through a horse-

---

* I think he added that, unless you postulate a one and
self-identical ego, or spirit, behind experience, no rational, con-
nected experience is possible ; at best you could only have
disjointed, indistinguishable blurs of feeling, even if so much
as that.

collar at an argument, or intellectual position is, perhaps, not quite the same as to turn, or carry it by storm. But Folly, like Wisdom, is justified of her children. So long as an intelligent public demands buffoons, literary, or otherwise, it will get them. The majority can laugh loudest, and their hilarity is contagious. If when a certain Prophet said those disagreeable things about a woman taken in adultery, some professional joker among the conventionally pious Jews had but thought of making a joke about His coat not being brushed, or His hair being unkempt, the multitude of hollow-holy people, indulging in a guffaw, would have gone away better pleased with themselves, and in a better humour with everybody else.

"But, stunned and bewildered between all these clever, if pretentious jabberings, characteristic of this age of confused and contradictory voices, I rushed out into the open, perhaps somewhat unceremoniously, and in my dream—

RAGNAROK.

"When I went from forth the hall I was bewildered,
Whirled as in a war of primal atoms,
While a cloud of buzzing theories befogged me,
Stunned, and flew in misted eyes of understanding.
Firm foundations of the old world were removing,

Shuddering under, involved in their death-throes :
Magnificent grey temples ever-enduring,
Eternal mid the mazy moil of mortals,
Holding far-withdrawn communion with stars,
In the refluence of the human generations
Ebbing, flowing, round their high abiding calm,
When the worshippers confidingly sought sanctuary,
Threw themselves with wild appeal before the gods,
Sudden yawning with grey walls to swallow all,
Bowed, and fell upon them !

    Young-eyed gods, ah ! ye were beautiful in May-
        time !
Now, in burning lurid gloom of dying day,
Ye are withered, looking old, and wan and weary,
While your pale priest mutters palsied by the altar,
Your altar hurled asunder with contumely,
And a roll of smothered wrath from underground !
Your wild worshippers entreat you at your shrine ;
But in burning, lurid gloom of dying day,
Lo ! ye reeling fall upon them !

    Bells clang jingling-jangling in the steeples,
Drunken steeples, flickering like fire,
Thunder rumbles in the dungeons of the earth-god
And the gaping earth gulphs all !
Lo ! the masquers, and the mummers, in confusion,
Hurrying panic-stricken through the highway,
In disordered gala dresses from the revel,
With the lions, panthers, horses from the show,

Shaking scared, with their man-tamers, while the flowers
Are strewn about the pavement where they fell
From the white hands of inebriates who threw them,
Mad with orgy, mad with joy!
Sinuous wine from tumbled goblet dyes the palace;
And the men want not the women any longer;
Flimsy booths of the gay fair are all awry;
No resounding more of brazen vaunting accents
From the humorous showman showing off the mon-
    ster;
The man of motley runneth swiftly flying. . . .
    Lo! the guillotine is reared! the tocsin threatens!
Men with rude gnarled arms, and rags, and gory
    bosoms,
Red and rough as dragons, butcher grimly. . . .
Earth, a Pandemonium. . . .
All an infinite flood of night, with ne'er a refuge,
A roaring, ravening flood, with ne'er an ark,
Nor a dove with leaf of olive!
Sick abortions of the maddened brain colliding
Grapple one another in the gloom,
Going under, with the drifting wrecks of empire,
Orders, faiths, and commonwealths that shock to-
    gether,
Mutually destroying, as the armed men
Sprung from dragon's teeth of old. . . .
O Ragnarok, O twilight
Of the gods, a world confounded!

STUMP ORATORY.

" Now it seemed that all was still again, and that I was making my way to Hyde Park. As I went, I found some refreshment for my soul; for a ruddy-faced, clear-eyed little boy in a blouse, who belonged to the upper classes, was acting a 'puff-puff,' blowing, putting one little fist before him for buffers, and twisting the other for wheels, running on before his nurse, and stamping his little feet. Then, again, a poor ragged urchin, with brown legs and arms, was turning a Catherine-wheel for a copper or two, while another stood, broom in hand, whining, ' Copper, sweep, please, sir !' Then there was a Punch and Judy show, before which a lot of little children were gaping in silent and open-mouthed admiration. They would reproduce the drama in their games, nose-voiced Punch and all, when they got home.

" On the pretty Serpentine swans and ducks were floating; prattling, delighted toddlers feeding them with crumbs. Boys were sailing toy ships, boats rowing up and down, some with happy lovers in them; the fine old trees wore their early green, and many flowers were out; the usual riders rode to and fro in the Row, and the usual idlers stared at them, while the carriages moved in their customary long streams, with the ordinary fine people inside.

"But I came now to an open space where crowds were gathered; here mob-orators swayed the surging throngs with contagious vehemence of words, and violence of gesticulation, like wind arousing waves to roar and destroy. One to whom I listened flattered the new king, *Demos*, quite as grossly as any courtier ever flattered a more old-fashioned monarch, and with about as much sincerity. The many-headed sovereign, moreover, appeared fully as gullible as the ruler with one head only—perhaps more. But the numerous heads of a hydra are less easy to get rid of by lopping than the single one of a higher animal (the amiable Commodus thought so). King Demos, however, is easily led by the nose with a little cajolery. The demagogue was inciting to violence, bloodshed, and plunder, men and women in rags, gaunt and famished, or idle, brutal, and malignant; another was giving stones (or plaster) for bread in the form of atheistic materialism, of the same quality as that of which I had been tasting a sample at the club; only rather more highly spiced with blasphemy and obscenity, to suit a rougher palate; indeed, a policeman standing by thought of running him in for it. Of course he had not thought of running in Mr. Cultus, the highly accomplished president of our literary academy—first, because neither he nor the magistrate could have understood that gentleman's refined irony, even if they had ever heard of him, or of his books ; and, secondly, because so rude a procedure might have seemed inapposite, and scarcely lucid ; for Mr. Cultus didn't brutally slay our gods with a bludgeon before the populace, but, with an esoteric smile, before a select circle assembled in an inner chamber, delicately opened a vein ; protesting the while that he had only taken them in there to wash their faces, cut their hair, and improve their general appearance. Nay, he had but given them a well-bred and demure kiss ; if thereupon the crude and sour-smelling mob, with ugly names, figures, and faces, seized and hurried to crucifixion, could *he* be held responsible? I trow not.

"The stump orator, however, of the dirty bristles, brute jowl, and bloodshot eyes, was screaming that next time the people had a chance they would not be so moderate ; all the accursed brood of kings, priests, and nobles, should be extirpated, not one be left to beget or bring forth young vipers ; loathly and obscene ecclesiastical bats should be hunted from comfortable clefts of darkness in obsolete old temples. And their works, too, shall perish with them! All monuments of art, ancient historical piles, with their archives, all palaces and churches, shall be burned, or razed to earth, and the site sown with salt. The vermin shall be destroyed, with all the accursed dens that shelter them! Hell-fire of hatred blazed from eyes and lips, like flames from charred and marred abysms, that have once been door and windows in a consuming and dismantled house. But although undoubtedly this man pointed to terrible evils, his remedies seemed mostly impracticable and in the air, while his spirit was but the ugly counterpart of the tyrant's own ; he sought to stir up mutual rancour and bad blood, while making unjust and exaggerated accusations, even committing the sin against the Holy Ghost by calumniating that gentle and ardent spirit of charity, which prompts nowadays many an honest effort to further alien good. Indeed, he seemed a sort of man-eating tiger transmigrated into human shape, and the fiends chuckled audibly when he had spoken. But doubtless he was well paid, and looked comfortable enough in his black coat.

" Now an Italian organ-boy with a monkey came near to listen. Suddenly the monkey leapt upon the shoulders of the demagogue, and chattered there, mimicking the man's vehement gesticulations. It was all up! The mobile crowd burst into guffaws of inextinguishable laughter, and after indulging in chaff and horseplay at the tribune's expense, melted away to witness the nimbler and more exciting acrobatic antics of a rival mountebank hard by. But the lover of humanity in a fury, descending from his elevated position, and having with difficulty got rid of the monkey, cuffed the little organ-boy unmercifully, as a practical illustration of that justice and mercy, the want of which, in a fine frenzy of virtue, he had even now so eloquently denounced in a selfish priest-hood, and a bloated aristocracy.

"'Make him a bishop!' said a wag, when one complained of a too zealous ecclesiastical reformer; and so, perhaps, if you could have seated this bitter revolutionist in the high and comfortable places he inveighed against, his tone might have undergone modification, and his native bile have found as much sinister satisfaction in denouncing denouncers. Did not Raoul Rigaud of the Paris Commune revel on the fat of the land when he could get it, or was he still as virtuously indignant with anything like fat? Footpads *in excelsis*, footpads with a convenient theory, lolling drunk on thrones, defacing, mucking, and making firewood of them, wrenching consecrated patens from off the altars, with bestial jibe, and carrying them in mock processions of monkey-mummers! Such is the monarch of many heads, with a minimum of brains in them. His cunning courtiers, his bear-leaders, moreover, have invented a moral basin of water for him, in the which, like Pilate, he may wash his dirty hands, and after that lustration account himself even praise, rather than blame, worthy! For they have discovered, and assured him that the thrones, honours, and better clothing of more fortunate men have themselves been filched from the people, wrung out of the bloody sweat of their enslavement, and ill-requited toil! In

that plea, moreover, one must admit some justification. Herein may be revealed to us, indeed, that
mysterious, incorruptible, inevitable Nemesis of the
gods, so sure, however silent and slow-footed! But the
instruments of Heaven's vengeance are not necessarily
guiltless. 'The Son of man goeth, as it was written
of Him.' Yet 'woe to that man, by whom the Son of
man is betrayed.' For because A robbed B, it does
by no means evidently follow that G may innocently
rob F, and that no injustice is done to the latter.
Otherwise, what human contract soever, what title to
property, or civilizing security for tranquil possession,
and peaceable living could be proved or regarded
as valid and assured? Yet this is the very first condition of Liberty, the safeguard, sentinel, inviolable
forecourt, citadel, and environment of human dignity,
self-respect, and self-development. Or shall two
wrongs, perchance, make a right? If common Con-
servatism be callous contentment, common Radicalism
is cruel envy. Nor am I·aware that this man was
especially kind at any time to *individual* organ-boys,
or any other persons who might happen to need him,
in the concrete, though rabid about the wrongs of
Organ-boy, and People in the abstract. Apparently he
preferred 'the People' to any particular person. Indeed,
he was violent in his denunciation of "pauperizing,"
and "degrading" charity exercised toward any dirty
and disagreeable individual Jones or Brown (*e.g.* help-

ing him fraternally to tide over a bad time, as we might expect him to help us, if he were in our place) just like any political economist; though fanatical in his devotion to Humanity with a big H. In the grand universal overturn, which alone could satisfy his ambitious aspirations, this particular organ-boy might happen to tumble uppermost, or he might not. At all events, somebody would, and not those who are uppermost now, which is the main object. His large and lofty soul could only expatiate in vast, unwieldy, theoretic schemes, that will not fit any actually existing circumstances; he cannot condescend to potter over, and tinker at mere petty particular cases of misfortune, or minister to individual necessities, as they present themselves—unless, indeed, some distantly-related third person, or some objectionable system may lend himself, or itself, to eloquent denunciation; a rich man, for instance, who, *quâ* rich, is necessarily a tyrant.

"I, strolling away, stopped to listen to a religious preacher — a stern, somewhat uneducated Puritan, holding up Jesus Christ, and evidently blessed with a strong personal love to Him. He seemed an earnest and true man, though one whose outlook was singularly confined. Indeed, the doctrine he preached was dishonouring to our highest idea of. God; while this life, as he represented it, became a poor and colourless thing, a mere low and squalid passage to another and better, through which we were bound to hurry, as it were, without looking about us, lest we might be tempted to linger; but this surely was an insult to Him, who had made it so large and rich and beautiful for those who have eyes to see. How, upon these terms, can we do our needful work effectually, with consecrating and quickening spirit, resolved to adorn and idealize every humblest nook and corner, reclaiming from evil, and claiming for God? As the delightful old religious poet sings—

> 'Who sweeps a room as for Thy laws
> Makes that and the action fine.'

If we are so dissatisfied with Earth, moreover, is it certain that we shall be any better contented with Heaven? The *spirit* of such religion is a wrong one. The bush always burns with fire, though only Moses may see it, and know the common earth for holy ground. God is here, as well as there. Sour, jaundiced, unwholesome, inhuman, and selfish is that gospel of seclusion and exclusion, that exhortation to busy ourselves about 'saving our own souls' from a threatened wrath to come. Election, reprobation, the total depravity of human nature, and everlasting punishment, throw very little light, at all events, over those terrible problems of victim and tyrant, undeserved suffering of the weak and innocent, that haunted, oppressed, and made me doubt of eternal justice. Rather these

K

doctrines make darkness visible by exhibiting in the
Eternal Abyss the monstrous Image of a Supreme
God, made in the lurid likeness of evil, arbitrary men.

"Sadly moving away, I noted a pale youth declaim-
ing and denouncing—quite as evidently sincere too.
The burning iron of cruel oppression, of dire misfortune—not all his own, but also of those dear to him—
that of the great dumb human suffering people,—had
entered into his very marrow; those terrible words of
his were charged with no insignificant anguish—ready
to lighten a devouring sword in the heart of society—
with no impotent and immemorable subterranean
thunder of earth-upheaving, righteous, and destroying
anger. A destroying angel he! an *Enjolras*—yet to
him few listened : men may listen, however, one day,
and that not distant, when opportunity has matured ;
and then, woe ! woe ! to the heedless, wanton, wicked,
oppressive city ! Evil voices chuckle amid the far-off
murmur and mutter of impending civic storm ! But
the holy angels also are invisibly near him, those
awful indignant ones, who opened the seals of Divine
judgment in the seer's Apocalyptic Vision. For if
Justice and Mercy will not work peaceably and
genially for reformation, the necessary work will be
done more clumsily, through earthquake and volcanic
violence. After all, the people at large have benefited
substantially even by the horrors of Revolution ; they
are emancipated, and growing, with whatever serious

shortcomings, and defects—the scars, wounds, diseases incidental to cataclysmal crisis, and interrupted, insufficient, inappropriate, unassimilated food. But World-education should now progress more quietly, with less of hideous, exhausting convulsion.

BEWILDERMENT.

" Then, returning in a maze, I met my comrades.
All of them have unaware grown grey ;
A little while ago, and they were youthful ;
It seemed as if a year had made them old.
Is the hour of former intercourse so far, then ?
But I am all bewildered with the change !
And though, indeed, I feel myself yet youthful,
I learn from them that I am growing old.
For they also look bewildered when they meet me,
With an air as if they wondered at my youth ;
Then with self-reproving I behold them,
Feeling ready to sink with them into night.
Young lithe forms, and fresh young faces move around
    me ;
I know how the time-torrent hurries all !
Again the earth appeared to shiver, swooning under,
All that hath been solid a mere cloud ;
I remembered how but yesterday I met them,
Whom we call dead, while we talked at the street
    corners,

Even here where we who name ourselves the living
Are conversing now : in glory flashing by me,
Lo ! the beautiful, the young with their light laughter,
The beautiful, the young, fulfilled with life !
Ah ! how gently flow the years of sunny boyhood,
Wandering they hardly seem to move :
Now swift runners, lo ! they jostle rushing onward,
Eager hurrying, hurrying headlong to the goal, . . .
Massy billowy water lightening to the fall ! . . .
And I hear a peal of bells from a near steeple,
Very like the peal of bells in my far home ;
A child again I wander in the woodland,
Pick the daisies, rove beside the water,
And my sister smiles behind her bridal veil,
Emerging from the chamber to be married,
She who lieth in her sleep below the hill. . . .
All the voices dwindle while I hear them,
The faces fade ; I know not whence, or whither,
Why, or how we travel in the world-show,
Doubt of now, nor understand before, and after !

BOOK V.

DISORDER.

BOOK V.

DISORDER.

CANTO I.—NATURE. THE SEA, AND THE LIVING CREATURES.

"THEN I thought, in the bosom of Nature, whom I love so, who has revealed herself to me from a boy, will I forget now the misery caused by human sin, hardness, indifference, and mad cruelty—forget these confusions also of poor human understanding, vainly endeavouring to pierce the darkness of a night un-assuageable by any star, troubled only, not illuminated, with sinister fires of wreckers along the shore, where human ravage lies tossing in the wild surge, ground to fragments on the iron rocks. And now I found myself by the sea.

The cliffs resemble a roll of long reverberate thunder,
Dark solid-bodied form of some rock-crashing peal,
Long reverberate roll of a loud tumultuous peal ;

They are a rampart round the pylon rent asunder
From the mainland by the might of yonder waves that
    steal
Slowly and surely in from where they roar in the
    distance ;
I hasten over the sand that paves the lonely court,
Pass through the giant pylon, and with a swift insist-
    ence
Climb rocks in front of the cave that is the Sea's
    resort.
Only He for awhile hath left His grand Sea-palace,
And I may enter, daring for a moment to explore,
Until anon beneath the Titan arch He dallies,
Ere He arrive to play with the boulders on the floor ;
Arch He hath hewn for Himself in scorn of our ron-
    dure of arches,
Tall, irregular, huge, in outline lightning forked,
While day and night He moved in four great moon-led
    marches,
And mouths of the foaming surge with the hollow
    mountain talked.
Was not the Architect Chaos? the storm's abraded
    edges,
Gloom-model after which He set Himself to mould,
Or the journeying billows' beetling, mountain-rupturing
    ridges ?
Old Chaos hath a genius primeval, vast and bold,
Who tints the windy walls with dim red rust, and gold !

When the Main is here at home his lucid halls are
    paven
With a foamy-veined, and shifting shadowed emerald ;
  When he leaves, the ponderous purple boulders are
    engraven
With fairy tales of the water by the mighty scald.
I bathe and wade in the pools, rich-wrought with
    flowers of the ocean,
Or over the yellow sand run swift to meet the sea,
Dive under the falls of foam, or float on a weariless
    motion
Of the alive, clear wave, heaving undulant under me !
The grey gull wails aloft ; he floats on the breast of
    the billow,
And a wet seal flounders flippered on a shelf of the
    cave ;
He knows well I'll not hurt him, brother of mine, dear
    fellow ;
His mild brown eye beholds confidingly and suave.
Yonder the mouth of the dark long subterranean
    hollow,
Where with a light in my hat I drove the birds one day,
Who seeing the narrowing end, and a swimmer per-
    sistently follow,
Dived unexpectedly under, and rose up far away !
  But the cavern hath awful tones, dull crimson hues
    of the henbane,
Blood-red, as ancient Murder had been hiding here,

So old and unremembered, gory tints of the den wane;
Nay, for a smell of slaughter haunts the antres drear!
I will not remember, I thought! forget by the brine
    that I love so
All the terror of human sin that made me grieve!
Ah! refreshed for a moment, how may I hope to
    remove so
From the wrongs of those, my brethren? 'tis but a
    brief reprieve!
I deem some Horror hides in yonder gloom of the
    hollows,
The surge returns to glut them somewhere near my
    lair;
And while the sullen sound my lone ear gloomily
    follows,
With some foreboding cold to gaze around I dare.
Oh! what are these at my feet? Ship-timbers, masts
    that are shattered,
In the howl of the hurricane, crunched on the iron of
    rocks—
And lo! 'tis a corpse in the corner, swollen, sodden,
    and battered,
Nodding, and tossing its arms with the swirl against
    the blocks!
For the Sea hath returned already, He enters the
    outermost portal;
Let a man begone, or drown, by the crag-walled
    vestibule;

Let him begone, or drown, by the echoing vestibule !

Ah ! 'tis the corpse of a boy there—hear the wail of a
mortal

Who weeps by a fire in a far land, and waits for her
beautiful !

The sea hath returned already; He laughs in the
outermost portal ;

He washeth over the boulders, thundering to and
fro !

Who are they that inhabit here aloof from the mortal ?

What awful Powers, indifferent to human joy or woe ?

Of Demiurgic Powers, afar from the man and the
woman,

Are these dim echoing chambers the mystical veiled
thought,

Indifferent, aloof, or enemy to the human ? . . .

How, then, are they a haven for minds and hearts o'er-
wrought ?

Ah ! many and many an hour in your sublime communion

I pass, O gods unknown, of ocean, wind, and cloud ;

I find profound repose, refreshment flow from the
union . . .

Yet, O my soul, divorce no sufferers in the crowd !

Nay, for I hear in the air that pestilence of the
voices—

And it is not all the gale, nor cry of the wild sea-
mew !

' Say what sinister joy, not man's this time, rejoices,
The loud, shipwrecking, murderous tempest-whirl to
    brew?' . . .
    Anon was changed the spirit of my dream.

CANTO II.—MISFORTUNE. ADVOCATUS DIABOLI.
    MAD MOTHER.

" How the sunlights quiver
   Upon the river,
   Flash out, are lost,
   On wavelets tost !
   Trees in ranks
   On verdant banks
   Trail their leaves
   Where water heaves ;
   A boat is nearing
   A mossy strand,
   Young voices cheering
   Are heard from land ;
   Musical bells
   Of a village steeple
   Flood hills and dells ;
   And a village people
   In bright array
   Await the young,

This morning gay,
Whose happy throng,
All pure and white,
With smiles of light,
In happy union,
For a first communion
Sail over the river,
Where sunlights quiver,
From vineyard-nested,
Calm, hill-crested
Hamlets fair
In bloomy air,
On the other side
Of the rippling tide.
The saintly father,
While they gather
Before the altar,
Well-nigh will falter
From fond emotion,
And heart's devotion;
Will give the feast
To elder and least,
The while they falter
Before the altar,
Fair heads bent low,
Young hearts aglow;
To the gentle Saviour
All life's behaviour

Commending humbly,
And praying dumbly
That He will guide
O'er life's wild tide
To the other side.
They are singing glees, they
Merrily dally,
Songs on the breeze
Float into the valley,
While bells are ringing
Musically,
White sail winging
Over the wave,
They laugh at the grave
Boatman wan,   .
Or a doubled swan ;
At a fleck of froth,
Or a drowning moth,
Their mirth flows on ;
Youth's fount of mirth
Hath a holy birth
From naught, from all,
From great and small,
Perennial ! . . .
But one who watched the bark that brought
Her child athwart the flood
Bent eyes a moment, while she sought
A favourite flower or bud,

To adorn the bosom of her daughter
Against the holy rite ;
And when she raised them to the water,
No vessel was in sight ! . . .
Only a weltering dark mass
Upon the blaze abhorrent ;
The youth that played on summer glass,
Death-gript now in the current !
Whether a sudden squall had caught
The bellying full sail,
Or crowding to one side had wrought
Collapse, and that wild wail,
I know not, but their joy became
One agony and terror !
While we may lay no more the blame
On human crime and error !
A moment since, their beauty dallied,
The dew of youth upon them ;
Then gasping, panic-struck, and pallid,
A cruel Fate fell on them !
The shadow of holy mysteries
Within the temple nigh,
Mellowing joy within their eyes ;
And yet they were to die !
Shrieking for mercy, help, they drown
In anguished Love's full sight ;
So Heaven sends the blessing down,
Our pleading prayers invite ! . . .

And now I hear the chuckling hiss,
'This is their first communion—this!
See the pretty white young faces!
These the All-Father's fond embraces!
Will you arraign mankind if these succumb,
Or old Dame Nature, who is blind and dumb? . . .
    Visit again with me the London garret!
Two parents, and five children have to share it:
Virtue, shame, modesty, may seldom come
To those who litter in this pleasant home;
But slow starvation always; trade is dull;
Work hard to find; live skeleton and skull,
With sallow skin stretched over, youth is here;
Old sacks for bedding, and how soon the bier!
One friend insidious in the squalid stye,
Leers—the gin-flask! What other friend is nigh?
But if to alleviate their want you fret,
Be sure grim Doom will circumvent you yet!
    Or come and note small children at the show,
Who watch intent the mummers to and fro! . . .
"Fire! fire!" we yell! See, see how panic flies,
Until the ways are choked with mad atrocities,
Well-nigh more murderous even than the human,
Almost too cynical for very man or woman!
Heaped and piled,
With agonies contorted wild,
Of many an innocent little child!'
    Then did they show me other dreadful scenes—

The dull blind tyrant, with his myrmidons,
Who stalks, and slays his nobler brother beast,
Warning off man, child, woman, blest with vision,
From God's fair mountainside, His gift to all.
Let him beware! red Revolution waits!
Ah! fertile lands depopulate for game,
The charred and ruined hamlet on the waste!
Where once throve happy families there skulks
Tyrannous Murder's blackened face; there struts
Decorous Infamy, close-masked in Law,
The gentleman evictor, who evicts
The dying babe, and its heart-broken mother,
With choked sob praying shelter for her child!
He spurns her, fires the sheltering hut; they wander,
Aimlessly wander up the bleak hillside,
Some wailing, some with vacant stare, and some
A silent curse in their wrecked hearts. . . .   Behold!
Upon the torrid sands of Africa
Innumerable bones of spent black slave,
Starved, buried quick, knifed, mutilated, goaded
By callous driver, women, children, men! . . .
    'I hope you like our pretty magic slides;
Earth is, in sooth, a very lively scene!
A water-drop beneath the microscope,
Where loathsome animalcules gorge and war;
One huge disordered order, shrewdly planned
For subtlest ingenuities of pain!
Well, and so we laugh one long laugh the more!

Grim Chance runs riot, drunken conqueror ;
He reels athwart the world's dim battle-fields ;
Purple his robe ; a dripping sword he wields,
While his pale horse's flanks are splashed with blood,
Gorged vultures flapping round him ; earth is one red
    flood.
And for what priests tell of a wrathful God,
Avenging ancient guilt, bale-fires like this
Accumulate more gloom in the abyss !' . . .

(Anon was changed the dark dream-imagery.)

MAD MOTHER.

" After moonrise in autumn,
    By a wandering water,
    When a half-muffled moon,
    Dazed in a cloudland
    Of wandering grey,
    Looked pale from the cloud,
    Dim branches uncoloured,
    In a line with the moon,
    Under, over the moon,
    Faintly repeated,
    A dark woven lacework
    In the wan wave . . .
    I heard a low singing,
    Thin, shadowy singing,

Unwordable woe,
A wail from the ruin
Of a heart desolated,
A mind out of tune,
As a wail from the wind :
A thin faded form by the pale flying moon,
A face with the youth faded out from the eyes,
From the wan, weary eyes,
Save for her not a soul !
Save for her, and a child,
Whom she held by the hand,
In the shadowy silence ;
But she ceaseth her singing,
Low saith to the child—
'Come along, dear, with mammy
Under the water,
The soft flying water,
The sheltering water,
The kind, hiding water ;
You are going with me !'
Then they went from the shelving
Low shore together
Into the water :
And the child little knew
Where he was going,
Only clung to the mother,
Deeming her wise,
Was she not ever

Wise for her little one,
Love for her little one?
Yea, Love is wise!
Ah! she was true;
But the woes of the world,
Driven home by the devil,
Had maddened her mind,
And the child little knew,
Knew not the mother
Herself little knew,
Even she, even she
Herself little knew!
So they went in together,
Mother and child,
Awaking the cloudland
In the wan water,
Awaking the moon.
'O mammy, how cold it is!'
'Yea, very cold, dear!
Only 'tis colder
Yonder on earth, love,
Yonder on land!'
A gurgle, a silence,
Low wind in the rushes,
Never note more of song now;
Nor mother, nor child knew;
Ah! none of us know!

CANTO III.—SATAN.

" Now again in the dreary blear-eyed room,
Where the poor boy lay murdered on the floor,
I find me ; and that white heap lies there yet,
On naked boards, life-crimsoned ; a thin fog
Of London fouls the atmosphere ; the pane
Only reveals red tile roof, and soiled chimney,
Through shivered, grimed glass ; in the room is more
Now than one body ; cold upon her pallet
Lay the dead maiden whom they starved ; and through
The door half-open I behold the child
Flit up and down, with those two heavy irons
Dragging at skeleton arms ; while yonder stark
In that dim corner stares a small drowned corse.
Loathly, unclean accouplements in air
Take hinted shape phantasmal, or withdraw,
Amid the muttering of wicked words.
　　I feel death-chilled from some strange, ghostly air,
And vital power drawn from me ; then rushed
A supernatural Wind of ample pinion,
That swooped, and wailed, and fell ; the affrighted
　　　chamber
Shuddered : I was aware of a dread Presence.
It seemed a pale mist nourished on my life,
Deadly miasm exhaling from my body,

Trailing now convolutions serpentine
Upon the floor ; a monster parasite,
It thickened, coiled voluminous ; and then
Rose solid, palpable, huge dragon train,
Towering high till it assumed a crest,
Human, yet half inhuman ; now it wavered,
As though in act to threaten with a fang.
All the dull-white showed clots of blood in it ;
I deem them mine ; and yet the Thing appeared
Very embodied soul of the vile scene,
Of all the loathly outer circumstance :
Whose human visage, livid like grim death,
Whose vampire visage, monster life-in-death,
Fascinates with an evil-glittering eye.
    And still a grandeur outraged, and defiled
Sat throned upon the ruin-countenance,
On the large god-front, broadly reared and high,
Like some pale crag, some temple wall, shagged over
With thickets of dull hair ; on loose lewd lips
Dwelt Cruelty, Pride, arrogant Disdain,
While hard Hate glared from cavernous green eyes,
Unchallenged owner, with immense Despair ;
Save when some lurid Passion smouldered sullen,
Or flared infernal ; yet withal in them,
As on the haggard, marred, and wasted cheek,
There reigned so absolute a desolation,
That Pity rose upon the night of Fear
And Horror, like a timid trembling star,

Venturing even here with her faint ray —
Now It assumed the guise of a well-dressed,
And cynic-sneering modern gentleman.
　　None could have told the age of the dread Thing—
It might have been or very old, or young—
Whose haunting set grey face
Is all one blight, and pregnant with decay. . . .
I can but grovel, cower underneath,
Spell-bound by this, more dire than the Anaconda.
What is it?　Cain, the murderer, the rebel?
Or legendary wanderer, Ahasuerus?
Or that Medusa fury's Gorgon-head?
Ahriman, Satan, Mephistopheles,
Arch-critic, nourished on belittlement—
Malign joy strength accords to impotence—
Or some projection of the worst in me,
Horribly thriven at a soul's expense?
　　I hear it breathe in tones sepulchral, low,
Some heart-o'erwhelming knolling of a knell,
Which maddeneth, like that torture of the drop
In mediæval dungeons on the crown!
Now loud with heart-cleft anguish, and despair,
Syllables poignant with the wind's wild wail;
Charged now with hollow mockery and gibe,
Thin, ringing false, blood-curdling, half a hiss.
Every malignant word deprived of strength,
Drew life forth, slow blood from the gladiator,
And fell like clods upon a coffin-lid.

I felt as though some fungus of the charnel
Were growing over my dim, withered heart.
    'You shall not have your child for all your pother,
For he is well extinguished ; so are these—
The happy children a fair accident,
And these an uglier—thus you say they seem
To you—yet they're congenial enough
To other folk—proverbially tastes differ !
Your vice may relish what their virtue frowns at,
The while your bridling virtue scorns their vice.
There is no right, nor wrong, nor heart in Nature !
She suffocates the miner in the mine ;
Earth yawns to swallow honest labour, tombed
Among the fallen stones of his poor home,
Slowly to starve there, inaccessible.
She shakes his roof down upon masquing Mirth,
And gaily-tripping Innocence, but dumb
And stolid stands, accomplice of a crime.
Who hurls the panic-stricken freight of men,
So roused from slumber, trapped in their own trains,
From high-built viaducts, their own proud work,
Ablaze, one shrieking, dizzying chaos down
To iron-bound winter water, which denies
A drop to quench the fierce flame, that devours
At leisure victims, caged behind strong bars,
Themselves devised to guard from misadventure !
Convulsed with mirth at her grim irony,
Look how she glowers over them, and grins !

What more? the time would fail me, should I summon
All my great cloud of witnesses for evil!
She grinds together huge ships in mid-ocean,
Mere brittle shells in Her portentous grasp,
Holds puny, pale crews drenched in cold suspense
Over the maws of ravening wave-furies,
That pluck and hiss at them, and show white teeth,
Where lurks the foul shark, ere she drops them in—
Maddens in open boats, until they prey—
Yes! pray to God—then prey on one another!—
Sun-smitten and delirious, after draughts
Of tantalizing brine from the false water. . . .

Huge ship dismasted, staggering to her doom,
While the loud surge sweeps over her drenched decks!
A man is lashed to the helm; the rest are sealed,
And battened down beneath, shut in with Horror,
To madden, rend one another, stifle, drown,
Rats in a hole; whose screams and wails appeal
To ravening wind, and wildly hounded cloud!
One plunge! one last loud shriek caught away by the
    blast,
Mangled, mocked, sucked into its mastering roar,
And consubstantiate with senseless Sound!
Dominant, blind black Vortex whirls, rolls, rages,
And brief-lived bubbles float in place of men!—
Dive to the deeps! there shapes of the well-loved
Drift heaped, stiff, festered, eaten of monstrous
    things! . . .

She decimates with cancer, and long pangs
On your sick beds ashore : O Tamburlaine,
Caligula, Tiberius, De Sade,
Well may ye droop your shamefast eyes, and kneel
Before your Queen, your Mistress crowned with crime,
Avowing how She dwarfs imagination
With hell-born ingenuities of wrong !
   Did God appoint the infant-murdering woman,
Who slowly starves, and rots with foul disease,
Through filth, stench, long neglect, cold cruelty,
Pale, pleading babes, she undertook to cherish,
Presiding genius of the baby-farm,
Vampire, that sucks the blood of innocence ?
Or did He make her heart, who does to death   .
Her own child, for some base insurance fee,
Which she will pour fire-molten down her throat ?—
Or doth this brittle, poor potter's clay defy Him ?
Our confraternity applaud such deeds !
But God ! Even I dare not so frantically
Blaspheme as charge such petty crimes on God !
If He commanded, then Myself am He,
And if permitted, He is Impotence.
Choose, man, your horn ! or else, renounce your God !
   Or will you, in sooth, sophisticate your souls
By arguing Wrong mere roundabout, masked Right ?
Well ! you are more mine for the specious lie ! . . .
If there's a God, I never met with Him.
The emaciate, cruel-eyed inquisitor,

And soldiers fanatic drenched earth with blood,
Oppressed the unconscious air with human woe,
In that dread Name! and who were glad but we?
   There is no right, no wrong, no heart in Nature :
Your right and wrong are rules for your own order,
Rules variable, moreover, and unsure.
Nay, virtue is but idiosyncrasies,
Similar, close-knit, long-inherited,
Thrust upon others, under penalty.
Provide for your own order how ye may,
Great Nature careth but a little for it!
Nay, but She made your order? Well, 'tis true.
Yet if you lean on her, you'll find a whore,
Fickle of humour, fancying one to-day,
And much preferring another by to-morrow.
Her rough-hewn plans jostle at cross-purposes,
Malformed brats, fighting as they leave the womb.
She shouldereth you unceremoniously
Aside in blundering on her big blind way,
And trampleth on the writhing hearts she whelped.
Hers the volcanoes, hers the foodful fields
They devastate ; who brings to birth fair children,
And loathly monsters, with the same set smile,
Vacuous, impartial ; now the Fury wields
Storm, Earthquake, Pestilence, now Human-thonged
Red scourges, Tyranny, or Revolution,
Lust, Murder ; yet She neither bans nor blesses ;
For Mind informs not the Automaton ;

One huge, impassive Immobility,
A Block, to whom Delirium lends gesture.
    Hers two colossal faces, and dread names,
Anarchy-Order, Order-Anarchy :
She alternateth both *ad libitum ;*
(Her seesaw is a trifle wearisome !)
    Whom She engendereth, shall she not destroy ?
Sole Fountain she of Honour and Dishonour ;
Absolute Sovereign, she may apportion either.
Who are you that arraign her ?   Pray, whine,
    whimper !
But, fool ! do you suppose that she can hear ?
Who wearieth more of babes and population
Than any murdering mother of you all,
Whom she inspireth in her irony
To emulate her royalty of wrong.

DETERIORATION.—I.

    " ' I commend to you the ethics of deterioration.
A genius, a temperament of fire,
Weighted with the dead weight of ancestral sin !
Pegasus turning a mill-wheel,
While his white wings wave, longing for the ether !
Yet even Pegasus cannot feed on air.
The portals of sense were closely barred
Against the entrance of any lovely vision,
Barred against fair imagery from the world,

Though the man was gifted with all sensibility.
Prepared in the stately temple of his spirit
Were niches for carven gods innumerable,
Who would have made it beautiful as a dream.
These by the Architect in irony,
These was it forbidden to fill in :
Night formless suffused the ample spaces ;
For the Builder had left the windows blind.
Within were all appointments for ritual,
Yet neither wrought gold, embroidered fabric, nor
     pure white lily
Might ever be conveyed thither from without ;
And so the temple rites were maimed :
Although friendly voices from the darkness,
Kindly accents of comrades were fain to cheer him ;
Yea, the voice of his well-beloved spake to him.
But one morning he addressed her,
Her blind lover addressed her,
With fond playfulness, as was his wont,
And there came no answer ;
So he leaned foreboding hands to feel for her,
To feel for her in her accustomed place,
Half hoping and believing she might be in play,
Because the alternative were too tremendous for
     endurance.
But her face was clay-cold when he touched it,
His consolation was clay-cold,
Who might have redeemed his soul !

A little later, the voices of companions,
One by one, were put to silence;
As lamps may be extinguished after service;
Until around the solitary inmate
Reigned one immensity of desolation.
   Then awoke the House-Curse of the family,
From where it slept in the dim crypt,
Feigning a mortal slumber;
It waited only for opportunity.
Now the Fury sprang upon him,
Seized him in his mortal weakness,
In the lone hour of his despair,
Gript him in relentless talon;
Till he, weary of unendurable
Life, yielded him to temptation,
Delivered himself over to fatal vice,
With unnatural lust wooing even Annihilation.
Then fell the fair temple, tottering to ruin.
   Have you ever watched a drowning thing in the
     water—
A little animal thrown into it by rough hands?
For a moment it struggles in mortal anguish;
But stone upon stone, well-aimed,
Sinks it with reiterated blows,
Mangled and choking, under the flood. . . .
Who weighted with ancestral ruin the feeble soul?
Who flung it in sunless gulfs to drown,
Stoning it with misfortune upon misfortune? . . .

But "*credo quia impossibile*,"
I may boast, has never been my motto !
"Hast thou observed my servant Job ? "
I think I may answer that I have observed him often.
And such was the conclusion at which he arrived.
So I leave you to conclude what was mine. , . .
Regard but the seething swarms of your huge cities !
Steeped in muddy environments from their birth up,
The stagnant sewer of whose blood is one corruption,
Dull reptiles nourished in congenial slime.
If there *were* another life beyond the grave,
These would enter it under favourable auspices !

Lo ! the blithe squirrel, with its nested young,
Who plays among lit laughter of young leaves,
His stored nuts of the forest lying near,
Suddenly troubled !—he descends the boughs,
Feebly resisting : at the caverned trunk
Arrived, there glare fixed eyes of a stark snake,
Ringed, mailed, fierce lusting for its proper prey,
Waiting him in the hollow : look ! he leaps,
Death-doomed and dazed, into red-gulfing jaws,
Inevitable—type of your free-will !
Example of the kindness of your gods !
And their beneficent contrivance ! fie !
What "good" can Horror do this animal ?
What "moral gain" to him in lingering torture,
Or long, excruciating agony ?
Glad life grows out of, feeds on, painful death . . .

Such the essential structure of the work
Omnipotent Benevolence devised!

These slaughters, and that roasting of a mother
By her own children for a paltry hoard,
Over a slow fire! yawnings of hell-fire,
Flame-flaps to show the furious furnace under—
A boy of eight, her grandson, told the tale—
What admirable nurture your good gods
Provide for their young charges, to be sure!
Old Priestcraft did this family much good!
Priestridden, Agnostic, ye are all one Death;
Your Calvinist was right at least in that.

Some are born devil, and some saint, they say,
While some born devil seem to turn to saint.
All by material necessity!
A brain secretes the virtue, and the vice,
Which, decomposing, can secrete no more.
And blood-disease, or blows upon the head,
Convert the sage saint back to a mad sinner,
For all's laborious goodness, built with pain—
That's a " conversion;" only upside down!
Nay, I've known many a hale old man "converted"
In such a wise, and cursing his pure youth;
Joseph regrets that wife of Potiphar,
And rails on the prim boyhood, which refused her,
Because he'll never get another chance.
The drivelling babe returns in the old dotard,
Fool's babble of man relapsing to the silence,

Whence it emerged so very uselessly.
Cease, vain curvetting Virtue! you who dance
As you are wound by the fool, Circumstance!
 The use of suffering! use of fiddlesticks!
See yon blasphemer harden under it!
And when primeval Chaos comes again,
The old Abyss remains indifferent.
If it's a comfort, pray to the deaf Silence!
But understand, it can't so much as grin,
To mock your prayer. And for your "wise," "good"
   men,
Who, fumbling at old knots, entangle more,
Who, wrangling, only pour oil on hot hate,
These are but bigger animalcules; all.
Your little noise will cease at the last cold.
The Deep once dreamed a nightmare of abortions,
The Tragi-comedy of Human kind;.
And when It woke, misshapen shadows fled;
I pray God to avert another, like it!
 Why did you leave your old glad gods? For now
They lie dead; yea, and younger gods lie dead.
Why stayed ye not with Bacchus and his crew?
Remains for worship iron-bound blind Law.
Ye move now in a dim, dun, dismal world
Of listless Wealth, of lean, monotonous Toil,
One bone between her savage and starved sons,
Snarling and tearing madly for one bone,
Who make the earth that groans beneath red shambles.

         M

There is no life for you beyond the grave,
No, nor redress, nor hope for these dead children.
Why crush your heart against the Inevitable?
Nay, rather, sip your pleasure—gulp your bliss—
Get all you can! enjoy it while you may!
Or if you say you may not relish joy,
Because it tastes of alien suffering,
As though some tears had dropped into the cup,
Then die! die now!   Repose is with the dead.
They have a monopoly of that!
And thank your stars, poor men, that ye are mortal!
What direr curse than immortality?
Than immortality without a God?
Alas! alas! . . .
Ha! what am I, then, who now talk with you? . . .
Why, a phantasm of your disordered brain! . . .
Mad! are you? . . . wish you may indeed go mad!
In such a world 'tis better to be mad.
Lie down with this cold clay you say you love—
What if some like their cuddles cold, some hot?
    Old age, the shadowy vestibule of Death,
Long, chill, pale cloister, over-roofed with yew,
Looms lone and dreary; Death awaits you all,
To still your tired hearts for you; then die!
Cut short the long unfriended road; die now!
Ye dawned at early morning from the Abyss;
Now it is evening; fade, and cease therein!
And learn, man! one dread name of mine, Despair,

Most formidable name of all the names
Men call me by !—more life but means more pain.
Then why live ?
That inner burden which you deem your sin
Weighs heavier, ever more intolerable,
Weighs you to earth, yea, drags you down to hell.
   You cannot carry it with jaunty step,
Or light heart, nor yet leave behind—how cure
The monstrous cancer of your own bad blood,
Anger, and lust, and vanity, and pride ?
Repentance ?   Had I any laughter left
I'd keep it all for that !   Repent !   To-morrow
You'll sin anew, and more yet !   Will remorse,
Were it sincere, undo the harm you did
To those weak souls, whom you dared feign to *love* ? . . .
   Ye are but attitudinizing apes,.
With all your airs of penitence, reform ! . . .
Why scold your fellows ? hypocrite, look nearer !
You, the potential murderer of these !
You, their corrupter ! . . . die, for very shame,
Before you inflict worse injury !   Begone !
Why seek not now the cold breast of your mother ? . .
I mean the Abyss, your mother, fool ! to rest
There from more conflict, effort, vain endeavour,
Even as they ? . . . So very still they lie . . .
Behold their slumber !—that is sleep indeed. . . .
Your child, your mother, summon you away. . . .
What ! don't you recognize the sainted tones ? . . .

Nothing is certain, save confusion . . . go ! . . .
Fall down, and worship . . . in me behold your god !'
I, cowering underneath the awful eyes,
Regarding, fascinated, the dread Face,
Whose stony cold invades my own chill heart,
Beheld therein, with more supreme dismay,
The same dire Visage, which confronted mine
Erst in my lonely thought, when insolent
I dared adjure great Isis to unveil,
And, for reward, beheld the countenance,
The rigid countenance of Death, that wore
Malign, set scowl of supernatural Hate. . . .
Methought this loomed more large, till it usurped
All space, and claimed to be the Universe—
Our flimsy decent coverings withdrawn,
Withdrawn   at   last. . . . 'Now,   am   I   fair?'   it
        breathed
In hoarse, low mocking tones . . . and lo ! this seemed
Mine   own   face,   dead. . . . Thrust   down,   I   reeled,
        and fell . . .
Yet clutched at somewhat in the jaws of hell . . .
Yea, nerved my spirit with one last wild cry
For one last wrestle with the enemy. . . .
A Voice spake in me ; yea, mine own heart spoke.
Ah ! but it sounded like his, who forsook
Our darkling path in that far-off drear night
Of winter ! and yet *I* cried out for light ! . . .

BOOK VI.

ORDER.

BOOK VI.

ORDER.

"AERIAL walls of our wide world,
Built round my heart, a stifling tomb,
I would ye were asunder hurled,
And yielded me a little room !
Yon ample air-dome of our world
Weighs on me like the ponderous lead,
As in a nailed-down coffin curled
I cower, alive, alas ! not dead !
For if my lambs must suffer so,
Fall on me, pillars of great Earth !
Or let me breathe, O let me go,
Where I may find for these new birth,
The wronged full-vindicated, blest,
And justice for the poor opprest ! . . .
The Heart disdains your message of the sense,
Demands the triumph of wronged innocence,
Demands to break up all the starry roof,

To rend and burn through yon ethereal woof,
Claimeth to breathe in a Diviner day,
Where all her winter buds will find their May.
Ah ! what inspireth faith, and hope sublime,
If not One throned above your space and time ?
Gleams in the cloudy darkness of His feet,
Who, crowned with stars, hath sent the Paraclete,
Dim, weary wanderings of our path to meet !
What ! if ambition, pride, lust, all my sin
Drag me from that high festival within !
Albeit I may never find the Grail,
Yet will I testify, before I fail,
Though from afar, like Balaam, all is well
With God's own little ones, with Israel—
Yea, for Sandalphon waits on the high stair,
Ushering to Heaven every humble prayer ;
While Jesus, Mary, rise to lead them there.

CANTO I.—HEAVEN.

" Then burst asunder prison bars,
Men name earth, ocean, air, or stars !
So to my inner sense revealed
A world their glory but concealed.
Like a pageantry of cloud,

Or enchantment disavowed,
Vanished, and were rolled away,
As a dream at dawn of day!
Laughing children, all in play,
Round one another veering flew,
Swift, dallying swallows in the blue,
While the pulse of their white wings
Made audible soft winnowings,
In many a threefold flower-cluster
Dewy-eyed, a pure white lustre,
Delicate shadow falling fast
From each on either as they passed. . . .
Joy! I knew them for the same,
Emerged from purgatorial flame!
Surely there I see the boy
One killed because he bought the toy,
And there the spectre-child, whose arms
The cruel double iron harms;
(Ever up and down the stair!
Nor Madness snatched him from Despair!)
These the little ones who starved;
One all unheeded, while they carved
Under her their toothsome meats;
These whom the hungry fire eats;
Yonder those hell-lust hath mangled;
And whom God's laughing water strangled:
The Holy Innocents! are they
In God's garden here at play?

Lo ! my little one among them !
Many lovely flowers he flung them !
Where are, then, the scald, the scar,
That may their beauty-marvel mar ?
All unremembered, transitory !
Yet a richer, rarer glory
It was theirs indeed to gain
From their crucibles of pain ;
From the bruising of the stone
A myriadfold the rainbow shone.
Starry gleams are in their eyes,
Lighted by no cloudless day,
A glory-glow of sacrifice,
Born of night, and pale dismay ;
A world of stars, a milky way !
Every child a Christ as well,
A Holy Babe of Raffaelle.
Are they dews in their soft hair,
The laughing irises at play ?
No, wild whirled wheels that never spare,
Like fierce attritions of despair,
Ground the diamond to spray,
For tendril locks a laughing light !
Red roses on their flower-white
Have fervent hues of human blood ;
Nor are they born of only light ;
Mother Earth, her lowly wood,
Fed them, our grey rain for food.

Then, with a fountain's delicate rain noises,
(A silver moss leaps plashing where it poises)
I heard afar melodious young tones
Of children, warbling limpid antiphons,
Of singing children, sister answering brother,
And flying, flying after one another.

FOUNTAIN SONG.

First. " ' Where is the rainbow ?
        Where may I find it ?
Second. ' In a fountain falling
        With the sun behind it ! '
First. ' Where the flying silver
        Falls loose, dishevelled ? '
Second. ' At an airier fountain
        Your look be levelled !—
        Where gems enhancing
        Aerial blue,
        Are glimmering, glancing,
        A delicate dew ! '
First. ' Come you, and show !
        I never shall find ! '
Second. ' Wait till he blow !
        Ah ! whims of the wind ! '
First. ' Silent in airy dew
        Playfully wafted,
        Rainbow, the fairy, flew

Swift from the shafted
Watery column !
He will beguile
Old over-solemn
Faces to smile !'

Second. 'Here, over the leafage
Glowing to golden,
Not for a moment
Will he be holden ;
A glamour of glory
Over the trees !
Ever murmuring story,
Low melodies !'

First. 'Now he is laving
Clear in the pool !
Wavelets are waving
Delicate, cool !
He is all azure,
Purple and yellow,
Following pleasure,
Beautiful fellow !
Awhile appearing,
Now here, now there !
Vanishing, veering
A Glendoveer !
Everywhere !'

Second. 'A bird who is washing
In a waterlily bath

A very fine flashing
Leaf-laver hath !
The young jet of joyance,
Clear with no colour,
Will yield all her buoyance
In a ruffling corolla,
Fall, a resolving
Soft silvery flower,
Woven water involving
Heaven-hues in a shower !
Deliciously dying is
Dear as the fleet
Swift thrill of flying
Morning to meet ! '

CANTO II.—HEAVEN'S MINISTRY.

" Then one of the fair flower-band
Led me gently by the hand :
Had I to choose among them all,
On him alone my heart would call !
Yet by my grief I was aware
Once more of our terrestrial air,
Of pestilential dens, where those
Grim horrors litter and repose.

I murmur 'Love ! need we return below ? '
'In heaven I am unhappy while I know
My playfellows in earth-life weeping so !
Ah ! when your anguished little ones are going,
We illume their way with gentle angel-glowing,
We tender visions of serene repose,
Havens from the weeping and the blows,
Hued like the rose,
Where a healing fountain flows !
Your mortal mind may never paint
All Love doth for them, when they faint ;
You divine not, you are blind,
Angel anodynes behind
Those outer agonies of dying ;
We wait invisible to soothe the sighing,
Till we may bear your ruffled birdlings home,
Where never hawk may come !
Poor earthbound eyes are native to the night,
Unapt to bear the dazzle of our light,
Familiar only with the realms of death,
Where many a formidable form drew breath ;
You only saw and heard the fiend ;
None of our cadences, who weaned
Your children from the breast of earth,
And fed with food of heavenly birth !
Yea, and we will arouse in very death,
That battens vampire-like on blood and breath,
A pang of life-revival, a faint qualm

Disturbing to the horrible cold calm
Of carrion conscience; till it burn remorse,
Under the hot accumulating force
Of righteous indignation breathed thereon,
Until for these, these even, be well-won
Saving damnation of the fiercest hell;
Heaven's own dread dawn, for all your bigots tell!'

Canto III.—Faith.

"Humbly I heard him, fair as morning-tide,
Whose high humility love-lore supplied.
   'The future generations of such men
Will marvel at what little moved them then.
Behold the gloom that hides the morrow parts;
And lo! well-tended homes, and kindlier hearts!
These evil natures, wandering astray,
Have only arrived less far upon their way;
And they must pass where they are passing now,
That through them world-experience may grow.
The Lord transmuteth leaden ill to gold
With all-compelling alchemies untold;
Œonial fire will melt the hardest stone;
By wave-persistence cliffs lie overthrown;
Through weathering circumstance high hills are gone.

What ! were you frighted with your own thin shadow
Adown the lawny, flower-illumined meadow,
Poor timid doe,
As you ran below?
Distortions of your short and feeble sight,
Calumniating our fair sons of light !
You feared grim idols your own mind had wrought,
Confusions of a miscreating thought,
Feared you yourselves would all dissolve and fade
In Time and Space, which ye yourselves have made?
Mere images phantasmal of the mind,
Who knows but shadows of true things behind !
Nay ! for the soul is mistress, and not slave !
Let her assume dominion, nobly brave :
For these, not she herself, shall feed the grave.
    The spirit of the universe will leaven,
However slowly, our poor earth with heaven ;
Only with ampler dawn of holy light
More sharply show the shadows of the night.
God's foes have grown more desperately bold,
Sore pressed, and driven to their last stronghold.
The bruising of the ground, the stern upheaval
Quickeneth germs of health, and feedeth evil.
Plant higher types, for these at length prevail,
Strong to extirpate lower growths of bale—
The Human deepens, widens evermore,
Till young Love reign from shining shore to shore.
    The general Soul, with hidden help from you,

Adapts fit frame for life-relation new,
Death's changed environment; Heaven will endue
With novel organ for communion,
Congenial with powers ye put on
For ampler knowledge—whosoe'er indict
That mellow wisdom of the Stagyrite.

CANTO IV.—HUMAN SERVICE. SONGS OF GOLDEN DEEDS.

" ' Now will I show true nobles of our race;
Let them those libels on mankind efface !

CHARITY.

" ' To dwell with evil loathed and drear,
High ladies leave their natal sphere,
To dwell where reeketh manifold offence
For delicate, well-nurtured sense,
Dividing holy heritage
Of inward treasure; there to wage
Deadly feud with the grim host
Of Satan, sharing all with lost
Wanderers in our wilderness,

Sallying to save and bless;
Yea, very bread of their own mind and heart
They break, celestial manna to impart,
Not hoard for mere "salvation;" gifts more blest
Than gold; faith, hope, and sympathy, with rest,
Strength, courage, wisdom, righteousness, and love;
They bring to earth health, healing from above.
We do not halve, we double what we share;
It groweth more substantial, and more fair,
More ours, for being theirs; (one family
We are of Him who is afar, yet nigh;)
Even as the widow's cruse of oil, or bread
Wherewith the famished multitude One fed.
Now rich and poor join hands; the air is still,
Saving for angels, singing "Peace, good will!"
Yea, one may deem it even the happy morn
In Holy Land, when our dear Lord was born;
And though the snow is on the ground,
Warm human hearts abound.
How dim soever, to be here is well,
Where these are making heaven out of hell;
Hark! merry peals of many a Christmas bell!
    Ding-dong-bell!
No more the evil ones low muttering talk,
For nigh the hallowed ground no fiend may walk.

GORDON,

"'Gordon, England's Red-cross Knight,
With many a dragon born to fight !
Great Gordon, waving a mere wand,
Rouses warriors who despond !*
With genial beam of his grey eye
Summons men to victory ;
Creates an army out of nought,
Unconquerables from hearts distraught :
His character, and equal laws
Enthrone secure the better cause,
　And now alone o'er desert sands
He rides to Ethiopian lands,
Where his mere presence is a spell
For yon dark race that loves him well,
Where righteous, simple, true, and brave,
Long he toiled to free the slave,
Tender as a woman, strong
As a man to punish wrong ;
Human lover, trampling self,
Scorning fame, and power, and pelf.
　Who, bursting on the boy of blood,†
Walled in with his man-murdering brood,

---

* In China.

† Suleiman, son of Zebehr.　See Gordon's "Journals" in
the Soudan.

A dark armed threatening multitude,
Slight, travel-marred, almost alone,
But leaning on the mighty One,
Dominated the fell clan
With a power Promethean,
Power of greatest over least,
Of human tamer over beast.

    Arrived, he welds to one strong blade,
Men disunited and dismayed ;
Burns the rods of tyranny,
Breaks fetters from captivity ;
At his well-loved name they gather,
Hail him Lord, and Saviour, Father,
Proclaiming equal law for all,
He bends to lift the weak who fall ;
That large heart holds the dark young slave,
And our white waifs beyond the wave,*
Whom he, delivering, with love
Follows whereso'er they rove.

    At sunrise how alert and eager,
Where the dusky swarms beleaguer,
Behold him from the palace roof—
Morn-flushed wave, and waste aloof—
Serene, yet anxious, watching Nile,
Where he winds for many a mile,
Surveying grim besieging host,
His rabble armed, and guarded post,

       * His Greenwich boys.

Waiting till the redcoats come,
To save his people in Khartoum!
Confronting cataracts, sands, rocks,
Thronged foes' indomitable shocks,
How they stem the adverse tide,
All British discipline, pluck, pride,
Panting to be at his side!
While England longs to rend the curtain
That shrouds her hero's fate uncertain.
Too late! the man deserted, fell,
Whom only treachery might quell!
Gordon, England's Red-cross Knight,
With many a dragon born to fight!

THE LIFEBOAT.

"'The manhood of your rugged coast,
Nelson's indomitable host,
Your manhood braves the raging seas,
Deaf to prayers of siren Ease,
Or warm Affection's humid eye,
To rescue shipwrecked souls who cry. . . .
Hoar ocean's wrathful night-usurping noise
Warns, like a dread god's doom-denouncing voice;
They lean athwart the solid wall of blast,
Blinded with flying froth from forth the vast,
That spits contumely from moving mountains
Of toppling water torn to foam-white fountains;

The maniac surge leaps furious while they launch ;
Falls a dead-weight upon the bark so staunch ;
But may not shake the mighty hearts that use
All strength of stalwart limbs and iron thews
To strain their oars athwart the swirling brine :
Big-booted, and large-chested, they incline
Broad backs together ! grim face and set eyes
Of coxwain fail not, nor strong hand that plies
Swift function of the tiller : how they bound
Up, down, abysmal cliffs of night profound,
That flash fierce scorn of them, engulfed beneath,
Hiss up to Heaven, and threaten with white teeth !
Hark ! through the storm-embroilment a faint sound
Of guns appealing ; piteous rend the sky
Red signals from the wreck's extremity !
    Their lifeboat battles with the wave ;
Grace Darling's countrymen will save,
Or perish ! . . . perish ! on the shore
They are thrown lifeless mid the roar !
Now mothers, wives, and children weep. . . .
All mothers, wives, and children weep :
All England bends above their solemn sleep :
Hear her intone their requiem full, and grand, and deep !

SEA KINGS.*

" ' Who are these three, that in a little boat
Have dared upon the Antarctic surge to float,
Journey from Durban round the Cape of Storm,
Which hero hearts again to-day transform
Into a promontory of Good Hope,
As when grand Gama, and Diaz did grope
Their all unknown dim waterway of old?
These Scandinavian mariners, more bold,
In a frail bark they hollowed far inshore,
Built from pitch-pine, and to the ocean bore,
In a frail open bark ten months will beard
Atlantic dark and formidable, steered
By their own sea-gnarled hands with dauntless strength,
Till they attain to our green land at length.
From where grim bastioned Table Mountain frowns,
And with the cloud his brooding forehead crowns,
To the caged eagle-emperor's arid isle;
By flowery Azores they rest awhile;
By Mauros, Corobeda, tempest-driven,
They arrive in England's welcoming white haven;
The wonderful heroic voyage passed,
Through all vicissitudes come home at last.
Ah! courage-consecrated little bark,

* See log of the *Homeward Bound*, exhibited at the Crystal
Palace on her arrival.

Men come to view thee, as wert thou sacred ark,
Or very Argo of the Argonaut!
With tokens of Sea's rough embraces fraught,
Rent canvas, cordage, bruised wood, plainly tell
Of rude storm-buffets; tangled weed, and shell
On keel and plank now long contented dwell!
By half-amused, half-indolent contempt,
Or admiration for the bold attempt,
Was Ocean held from drowning the three men?
Rather the God they worshipped in His ken
Kept, gave swift vision, accomplished craft, with power
To stem, surmount, and baffle danger's hour.

O'er beetling cliffs of water, lo! they bound;
Engulphed now in a reeling chasm profound,
Obscure, foamed, swirling; storm-breath on their side
Lays them, and plays with them; and yet they ride,
Storm-seasoned hearts of oak, on the wild tide!
Endurance, vigilance, strength, iron nerve,
Tense, ne'er relaxed, allowing none to swerve
One hair's breadth from his function, even for stress
Of wet, cold, hunger, thirst, or weariness,
Strain unrelieved on every faculty!
If caught off guard one moment, they shall die!

In peril from the monsters of the deep,
In peril from wild, ruptured surge's leap;
Fierce blast drags down, ere they may reef the sail,
Wave's weight half fills the hollow pine, bids bale
For very life, yet never great hearts fail,

It blew great guns ; stars blinked, and were blown out,
Or re-illumed ; they saw the raging rout
Of billow smoking skyward ; squall-slung spray
Smote, stung like hail ; then louder than the roar
Of breaker thundering on a rock-bound shore,
A sound more terrible than aught before
Appalled their ear ; some supernatural scream
Advanced toward them through the drifting steam :
And they beheld prodigious ocean herds,
Whales spouting geysers, porpoise, dolphin, birds
Rushing in headlong wild pursuit of shoals,
Menacing wreck, so hurling to their goals !
Buffeted bows "drove piles" in the hard sea ;
Storm, waving vast vans, howled tumultuously.

Dies from the cloud-range conflagration red,
And from long roller, taking hues of lead,
Sombre, oil-lustrous, fading dun and dead.
Cloud-mountains massed on pale horizons lower ;
Grim monsters follow, hungry to devour.
One all unknown, and horrible remains
Beside them, while blood-chilling twilight wanes,
Huge, livid-backed, dim welters, and to mock
Their own mast, two long spectral rods that rock
Protrude in polished outgrowth from the spine :
Sinister, *that* lurks near them on the brine !
While on their masthead sits a weird wild glare,
Like Death's pale lanthorn : ha ! what doth it there ?
And what is that, which writhes upon the bare

Pole, like what writhed upon the lance's head
Of Dürer's knight, on his faint war-horse led
Into the forest gloom by Hell and Death?
What means the Portent? doth it breathe life's
    breath? . . .
    Immured in deep night the world seems to be,
Save when flashed flame lets out the boiling sea. . . .
    But in long languor of clear ocean calm,
When the loose tiller held in listless palm
Made easeful noises with the lapping wave,
Dear home-thought stole upon the heart so brave;
While loved familiar constellations rise,
When they draw nearer native Northern skies;
High planets hold communion with them,
Pure worlds arising from heaved Ocean's rim;
Luminous lives, how still and soft they move
In the grey wave, akin to stars above!
While elfin phosphorescence from the prow
Slopes in two murmuring widened folds below.
Or in blue day the momentary gem,
Lovelier than a fairy diadem,
Twinkles innumerable on the rolling
Blue billow; yellow birds for their consoling,
Pale yellow, flying o'er the lisping foam,
Alight upon the ocean-cradled boom;
The gentle giant Olsen fondly feeds;
Till they, relying on his kindly deeds,
Perch on his shoulder, lilting blithe and gay,

Who sorrows when he finds them flown away.
  Often before a merry breeze they flew,
A wake of simmering silver in the blue;
Many a nautilus with filmy sail,
And fishes panoplied in rainbow mail,
And flying fish with blithe young hearts they hail.
Or ample-pinioned, gleaming albatross,
Swooping and circling, dipped in soft sea-moss,
Then sunward soared, on calm, unwearied wing,
With plaintive white mew, air-meandering.
  Alone upon the inward-murmuring sea,
Alone with God in the Immensity!
With worship, pious, temperate men, they call
Weekly together on the God of all.
  Kingcraft, and overlordship of the seas
From Olsen, Nilsen, Bernhard, such as these,
And their Norse kindred, Nelson, Franklin, Drake,
For men of other blood 'tis hard to take.
They prove the race of heroes not extinct,
By whom our common-seeming years are linked
To those that loom more fair in the dim past,
When Gama loosed his canvas to the blast,
And Raleigh in strange waters anchor cast.
  Not ease, but hardship, suffering, privation
Root, toughen, hearts of oak, and mould a nation.
Bear witness Holland, Athens, Albion!
Columbia, Teuton, Italy, made one!
By toil, and strife, and agony 'twas done.

The Isle of Lepers.[*]

" 'An isle of lepers ! perishing in pain,
Exiled from happy hale men ; Health is fain
To banish from her loathed Contamination.
Yet a priest-hero of the gallant nation,
France, saintly even as their priest of Ars,
Or him who shineth, an immortal star
In the grand page of Hugo, her grand bard,
Named Myriel, shrinking nerve will disregard
For love of God, and of our human kind.
Deep pity made insensible and blind
To natural aversion, mortal danger.
Following One born in the lowly manger,
He shuts himself from all he held most dear,
A minister from dreadful year to year
To men deserted, loathed, weighed down with grief;
Abandoning all that he may bring relief.
Unscathed himself for years, the foul disease
Hath eye malign upon him, and will seize ;
Hath claimed the high redeeming victim now,
Through whom your poor world will more god-like grow !

* An island in the Pacific. Father Damien is the priest's
name.

"WEAK THINGS OF THE WORLD."

"' A Christian convert, a boy-African,
Knowing the bloody lord of his great clan
Sought him to visit with a lingering death,
Because he had embraced Christ, humbly saith
To a revered white teacher, urging flight,
He may not bend his soul to feel it right;
For since he hath been commissioned by the king
Ingathered tribute of the tribes to bring
Home to the sovereign—coin of cowrie shells—
Whatever cruel personal peril dwells
Among those evil courts, how dare he thrust
From him the fatal honour of his trust?
And so he braves the tyrant; ah! young black,
Spurned as inferior, thou hast e'en put back
Poor human nature on the pedestal,
Whence pale dishonour dragged it to base fall!
The lowest, whom men trample like the clod,
Is of the royal family of God.
The humblest woman sits enthroned above
The wise and proud by dignity of love.
Who liveth well alone hath found the key
To every dim mind-baffling mystery.

* The Rev. Mr. Ashe, missionary to Uganda, related this
to me.

WORLD-PROGRESS.

" ' Enwombed in your imperial race
Fair organizing virtue trace,
To one great arbitrating nation
Moulding you by federation
Of kindred peoples for defence,
And high world-vitalizing influence;
While in the purple pomp of war
Dawn lovely hues unknown before,
Iris-hues of mercy mild,
An arc o'er livid flashes wild,
Born mid ashen mists that loom
'Thwart thunder-mountains in the gloom.
Patience, Fortitude, Compassion,
Woven i' the awful storm of passion
On wrath-rent cloud, are only born
Of rays that marry rains forlorn,
Of Heaven, who weds the Earth you scorn.
Beyond high service war may render,
Himself hath lineaments more tender,
Whose very terrors wear a smile,
Now Mercy doth his frown from him beguile,
Sweet Sister in the hospital,
Who vermeils with ethereal
Hues the cloud of wound, or fever !
Her angel ministration never

Faileth ; hurt weans of our city
Lie patient in her gentle pity.
Yea, Dora, Florence, all your sisterhood
Render illustrious our flesh and blood ;
    Ye twain appear ensphered aloft, afar,
In sorrow's Night, a luminous twin-star !
Spring, summer, autumn, winter drear,
Are needed to fulfil the year.

MOTHER'S LOVE.

" ' She had tended, done her best to cure him ; now
The little child of white and anguished brow
With her good will is nursed in hospital.
Clad in worn withered weeds, she brought her all,
And left the cherished burden ; she will start
Out of her brief and broken sleep ; her heart
Still seems to hear him call to her, and moan ;
She flies to help, forgetting he is gone.
Now since herself no more may slave for him,
Dull daylight, rainy, chilly evening dim,
Behold her underneath the window near
The little cot, where she hath left her dear.
She stays there till the allotted day for friends
Arrive, the hour that makes for all amends.
Every misty morning sees her come
From the mean alley, now no more a home.
Nurse, looking often from the ward, descries

The wraith-like face with upward-seeking eyes,
Haunting the wall; they wonder how he does,
The ailing child; but when at last she goes
Within the ward at the permitted hour,
She dare not ask for news about her flower,
Before she reach him, lest the word be spoken,
Which, falling on her heart, would leave it broken.
    Love blooms more large in yonder world of bliss;
But Love was nourished on the tears of this.

JUBILEE, AND THE GOOD EMPEROR.

    " ' Behold an empress-queen, who nobly reigns,
And an ideal womanhood sustains
Upon a throne, who wisely rules by laws,
From long deliberation, clause by clause,
Grown fair, and growing, fed with patriot blood
Of Tyndale, Hampden, Sidney, and the good
Martyred, unnamed illustrious multitude.
Her fifty years of dedicated toil
To all self-pleasing tyrants are a foil,
Who only nurse their poor prerogative,
Whether the starving people die, or live.
Her large, full heart goes forth to all that mourn,
Itself, alas! wrung, lacerate, and torn.
Our monarch hath a grander coronet
Than any mighty predecessor yet,
With many a subject people's jewel set.

First, orient India, fount of morning's beam,
Realm of the Avatâr, and wondrous dream !
Australia, young with earth's glad primal power,
Who weaves weird visions in her lonely bower,
Arms for defence her well-knit, stalwart sons,
And launches navies, iron-mouthed with guns,
To assure the Mother-mistress of the seas
Dominion more unchallenged over these !
In you, blithe land of long lake, frost, and fur,
Vast volumed waters of St. Lawrence pour
Their foaming thunders with an ocean roar !
All ye sent children armed for many a mile,
To help us nobly by Egyptian Nile.
Court gentle Peace ! and yet be well prepared !
Without our England, ill the world had fared !
Arm ships and soldiers ! ill may they be spared !
Distrust world-citizens, who fain would loose
Thine argent armour, deemed of no more use !

And thou, dark Afric's tempest-beaten Cape,
Around whom Gama dared his course to shape,
Sublime sea-comrade of Columbus bold,
By perilous water-ways unknown of old,
Thou, in the crown a diamond-beaming star,
Art sending sons to jubilee from far !

The pageant of her triumph proudly shone
With warriors, led erst by Wellington,
And that Black-armoured Prince ; red, sable, grey ;
Plumed horsemen, helmed, with steel and colour gay,

o

Swart Indian, jewelled in dim gold array;
Elect Colonial, powerful of frame,
With nation-founding faces, known to fame;
From every quarter of the world her guard!
Whose people throng the chariot way; they ward
Her throne from danger; love is great reward.
Bending with royal grace and beaming eye,
Moves the good queen, whose name is Victory.
The stately triumph of her glory moves
With loud acclaim, upborne by all the loves
Of all the people; kings and princes ride,
Her escort with no ill-beseeming pride;
Her chariot rolls, surrounded by her sons,
Of whom the nobler, grander port he owns,
Who wedded England's daughter; who will be
Magnanimous Emperor in Germany;
He, though great empire his mild rule embrace,
Hath character more lofty than his place.
  Here towering with eagle-crested casque,
Face, form, proclaim one born for his high task.
He, a more gentle, just, God-fearing Saul,
Hath waged grim conquering battle with the Gaul;
Will wage a deadlier with the dire Disease
That lays him low; yet, scorning his own ease,
Conquereth here too; patient, cheerful, brave,
While borne in strong midmanhood to the grave,
Bends calm, composed eyes on the public good,
Who in his long death helps the multitude,

Country, and well-beloved; who will not swerve;
For if Death numbs the right hand, left will serve;
But when one symptom "*apathy*" they named,
Then all divined that Death at length hath claimed,
If to the lover his dear world grew dim!
A Light and Hope of Europe quenched in him!
Alas! for her, to whom he gave white heather,
In Caledonia, in blue lover's weather!
He lies in state, he lies in his long rest;
And she hath laid the sere wreath on his breast,
Laurel, wherewith she crowned her Paladin,
In war proved, as in peace, a king of men.

Our queen moves royally to Westminster.
Fortune hath dealt in gracious mood with her.
Yet one irreparable bereavement laid
A scathing hand upon her heart! Snows weighed
Heavily, fallen from careladen years!
Changed, since that early hour of April tears,
When young-winged Morning in the minster shone,
Illumed with Heaven, her, wearing earthly crown;
Changed, since her marrying the wise prince she lost,
Before chill autumn, and the winter frost! . . .

But the broad highway laughs with various hue,
That seems to pour from forth aerial blue:
Roof, balcony, door, window, all the street
Teem with a happy people, fain to greet
Her, whom the loyal, glad, tumultuous sound
Doth welcome, Love's loud answering rebound

From her Love-loyal reign, re-echoing round ! . . .
Yet if this monarch were not good and just,
To Heaven the pageantry were only dust.

CANTO V.—WISDOM AND WORK.

DETERIORIATION.—II.

"'Did the fiend overwhelm you with deterioration?
Deterioration is a mystery ;
Yet none descendeth below the appointed deep.
Henceforward the way mounteth upward ;
It is darkest ere the day dawn.
For none fadeth away into nonentity,
Nor doth any carcase fester, unmitigated defilement.
The fiend ignored, having blinded himself, a core of
    soundness in the prodigal.
He feigned that all was dead ;
Being Death himself, he could feel no life around him.
Yet cheerfulness and amiability were well ; good also
    were generosity and patience.
These qualities rejoiced the heart of his friends.
Now surroundings more favourable being provided,
Where germs of excellence may awaken,
The passion-driven may possess himself at last.

Enthralled and goaded by the slaver,
Cramped and grovelling in low dungeons,
He never straightened himself to his full height,
Nor looked around him to far horizons;
Hindered, attained not his full stature—
His were no opportunities for development;
Never for a moment was he a free man;
Free to realize individuality.
Be sure the Universe needed the dread experience;
He was a scapegoat for Humanity:
Moreover, he was endowed with genius;
And her royal gifts are gain—
However terrible the price paid;
Whatever roaring gulfs the diver sounded,
He emergeth with a pearl of price;
And for that let us be thankful!
Offerings laid at the world's feet, they are the world's;
Yet returning into his bosom, they are his also,
Yea! his own for ever!
For he and the world are indeed one.
The destructible shall be destroyed,
Consumed with ineffable anguish,
And the unessential die.
But Individuality transformed
Will rise regenerate from the ashes,
Ideally-moulded, fair.
Or when doth God cease to heed,
To yearn for whom He foreknew?

Sending to earth a chosen messenger,
Cease to yearn for His bosom-friend?
Nay, but all souls lie in His bosom;
Verily they are His children!
What though the mortal loitered,
Frail tongue faltered in delivery
Of the message thereto entrusted,
Will Love hate, therefore, and forget?
Omnipotence own to failure,
Or impatient Justice break her tool,
Fling aside what herself hath fashioned?
Will God change like men?
Fickle, irresolute as one of you?
Whom He loveth He loves for ever,
And will heal the hurt of His lamb.

Did Satan tell you Nature made the man?
Nay, rather, God in man hath fashioned her.
To these, whom he averred that Nature slew,
Or cruel men, but whom we say God called,
Since they who die are only half in Him,
And half without, Death turns one pale dread face,
Yet shows another mild and merciful;
For Death is ever in the line of life.
Anomalies pertain alone to sense;
Yea, even to fairies of the fur and feather
Death is new birth to a life beyond,
Subserveth life; the spirit travelleth,

Through lower lives, to manhood, and yet higher.
Were there no God, or were the God malign,
Child-mirth and lark-song were impossible.
    Hath not the World-Soul fallen from his height,
His height of native Virtue, fallen low,
To sin and suffer, with the souls in him,
Who are ourselves, and every animal,
Divergent, battling, erst one harmony?
And they are elements within the Human,
Dissonancy clashing in the man,
Fallen, that all may rise to altitude,
No otherwise attainable, I ween.
Now every lower life may climb, through man,
To angel, dowered with experience,
How else to be assimilated? Wherefore,
In yon dim realms of feeling under us
Confusion reigneth; creatures are at war,
A mutual prey; disorder rules, and death;
The strong wrest breathing-place from feebler lives,—
Till Bouddh, with free will's high prerogative,
Feeds the lean mother-tiger on his body,
And, dying, brings the very Life to birth:
Now Justice, Mercy, dawn in the wild waste.
    All, sons of light, will form one Harmony,
Mutually permeable, cells
Functioned to serve with punctual, never-failing
Service the Body, never isolated,
False selves, to alien injury; one only

Orbs to his own completeness in another.
Then each will labour for the common weal,
Aware the commonwealth hath nourished him,
Laid fair foundations for his energy,
With free environment ; one breathes for all
Inevitably ; now with glad intent.
If each divined with kindly fellow-feeling
Alien need, and thirsted to supply,
Justice and Love would change your earth to Heaven,
And hallow poor relations of mankind ;
All human impulses were innocent,
And spontaneity benevolence.

All, sons of light, will form one Harmony,
Obedient orblets in their natal Orb,
Every one mirror, minister to other,
Warbling melodious in fontal spheres ;
We in our Mother Earth, the while She sings
Herself, with sister worlds, around the Sun,
And He, in his own course, obeys Another :
Beyond all moons, and suns of sense abideth
One Lifegiver invisible : the lion
Will lie low with the lamb, sublimely calm,
His lightnings veiled, his thunder laid to rest,
Strength couchant, folding meek Humility ;
A little child, with tender eyes, will lead
Them both to Eden-lake at evening-time.

Yours will be world-pervading faculty,
Known only now so far as fugitive

Aroma rising in the dewy dark
Of night may tell a tale of breathing flowers,
Who laugh illumed with morning, blithely fair,
Or as the drowsy bird who dreams and stirs,
And twitters in the woven nest ere dawn,
Foretells full choir, awake in the clear sun.
Earnests already of earth-emancipation,
Presaging a more ample life than yours,
Open around, with sheath-dividing gleam
Of diffident warm colour, vivid hues
Of slumbering summer; so the chambered cave
Allures with twilit possibility.
Body and soul, evolving many folded,
As germen, embryo, shadow what will be,
In ever complicating miracle.
Doth Nature lure her children with vain vow,
Hope hollow, longing ne'er to be fulfilled?
Only in seeming; for her satisfaction
Is ever more than of immediate want;
Only in seeming; she withholds to grant;
Her mandate is upon you; build your nest
For mottled ovals yet unmoulded; winnow
The air with wings for lovelier lands afar;
Find other lands beyond the sundering sea!
    Earth, air, and water are alive with voices,
Though men are only aware of a poor few.
The many aisles of forest, rapt by day
To deep dread silence, roars like ocean loud,

For other ears more sensitive to sound ;
Although no Storm descend in his hot wrath
To lay a violent hand upon their pride,
Nor, with the stress of his enormous weight,
Strong swoop of his immense and monstrous vans,
Swaying huge boughs to writhen agony,
Their foliage streaming as in a flooded torrent,
Hounds on Confusion—all the leaves wild whirl,
Trees creak, scream, shattering, ancient towers up-
     rooted—
By night beasts battle, bellowing o'er crushed prey !
But, even in the hush of sultry noon,
There is a Babel hum of population
From dense tribes of inhabitants that swarm
Through bark and leaf ; the velvet moth that flits
By twilight sings like birds ; fine ears will hear,
While vision banquets upon hues unnamed,
Marrying sights and sounds for a new world.
   Well-wedded worlds are mutually involved ;
But though the Centre radiate through all,
Yet are they mutually impervious
To any but a few inhabitants
Of either ; but in trance the soul may burn
From sphere to sphere, and find a home in either ;
In trance profound the soul is free of many,
Remembereth what she lost from memory ;
Some long secluded chamber of the Past,
Experience obliterate, remote,

Whose windows are unbarred again to light.
Light leaps to illuminate the annihilated,
Forgotten, dark ; for Spirit, after death,
From vantage-ground of her eternity
Proudly resumes her ante-natal sphere,
And blends with earth-life ; her young eagle vision
Surveys the suite of halls palatial,
Once more reclaimed for knowledge, where she swept,
Moved with her beautiful, imperial train
Of fair and noble faculties, from life
To life, a never-dying Queen divine,
High throned, in glory, above Space, and Time.
    Ponder the holy hieroglyph of Pain,
That hideth a high meaning ; Christ endured,
Hoping for joy of world-redemption, wrought
Through crucifixion ; are not all the Christ ?
Who wail, unknown their grand prerogative,
But, when they are crowned, feel leap in them the virtue,
Conceived anon through mortal suffering,
Then they exult, oblivious of the woe ;
Earth a dim moment in their never-ending,
Irradiate career from heaven to heaven.
Whose virtue (for the human race is one),
A virtue sinewed from the strife with evil,
In time will heal the human family,
Full orb the grand Atonement of the Lord.
He, with whom myriad years are as one day,
Beholds men through the well-beloved Son.

Pause; nor presume to wrench by violence
Flower from bud; await the month for bloom.
  The Deep is only Wisdom dark from depth:
We lose our lower lives indeed therein,
Only to find the higher lives we lost. . . .
How do I know?   One gave to me the vision!
Blest are the pure in heart, for they see God;
Galahad saw Him, even Percivale.' . . .
I felt the fiend gone from me; for the child
Rebuked him, like the lifting of the cross.
'O not without the sorrow, and the sin,
May be our human pilgrimage?   Ah! why?'
'And what if God Himself hath life by these?'
He answered, with a shadow on his joy,
Musing as though bewildered; then resumed—
  'What is your Faith? a hand that feels the Hand,
Which ever holds it; numb are all beside;
Yea, many of you are numb, and deaf, and blind.
A woman loses children at one swoop!
(I find her in the hovel, in the palace;
I find her in the fanes of all the creeds,
Yea, drifted in the sands of ignorance)—
A woman loses children at one swoop;
The wave, engulphing all, rejects her only,
Flings her alone upon the unchilded shore;
The mother loved them more than all the world,
More than her own self . . . doth she smile? . . .
      she sees

With far-away, sunk, visionary eyes,
Or inner eyes, that lend rapt air to these,
Them all reposing on the heart of God,
Yonder, as here, and they are with her still,
Because herself reposeth with them there,
Upon that heart; then wherefore should she weep?—
Her faith, the world-o'ercoming victory!
She is among the cloud of witnesses,
Who testify poor human weakness can
Smile in the face of dire Extremity,
Because she recognizeth her own Father,
However closely-veiled! our children trust
Our poor love, though, alas! we fail them oft,
Confounding ours with that great Love behind. . . .
   Notes of a singer soaring into heaven!
They seem to mount on ample, unfolded wings,
Like some white bird, who, joyful, breasts the blue,
Or undulate, frail boat upon a billow;
They are rays of light, aslope on a mild cloud,
Or doves, who pulsate, gleaming to and fro
About the carven cathedral front of Rheims,
Thwart silent, old-world, visionary glory
Of shrined saint aureoled, kings robed, and weird
      forms.
Now we are ware of dawn among pure snows
Of mountain mystical; keen flame divides
Our downy vapours, and pervades their grey;
An upward-mounting beam, that shines from earth,

Arriving at the very heart of God,
Swiftly arrives to nestle there at home,
Disclosing Him a moment with no veil
To our dazed wonder ! seraphim are flying,
Expatiate in blue celestial air,
Alight, wave wings from radiant promontory,
Clash, mix, confound their raptures in mid-heaven !
And now a gentle languor fades the strain,
Fallen gently, like a feather ; but in yon flashed
Ecstasy did you not surprise your lost,
Reposing happy in the fields of Heaven ?
And tell me ! do you deem such sounds could soar,
And wake such dreaming, if one tortured child
Had but one life of want and anguish given,
Then foundered in the void ?   It could not be !
Might such a strain indeed afford such vision,
If God were not, or did desert one child ?
If this were more than seeming, all would wither,
Core-eaten shows of the false world fall in !

CAGED LARK.

" ' Hear the çaged lark, athrob with the swift song,
Who floods our sense with notes, a hurrying throng !
In spirit, doth he bathe in the blue day,
And soar away
Over the dewy woodland, and green field ?
Or doth he fancy a sweet nest concealed.

In the warm turf, a downy mate, and brood,
While he finds food ?
Blithe captive, seems your prison ample, fair,
Free voyage in illumined realms of air,
Buoyed on your own full tides of happiness ?
Dear bird, we bless
Your glad content ! poor feet on a soiled sod
May never rise ; and yet *you* rise to God !
Ah ! mortal men may feel, confined to earth,
Faith's morning-mirth ! . . .

What work is thine ? to mirror in thine art,
Though feebly, as One may the power impart,
The human Quest, the Age's mind and heart :
While Nature doth her lineaments uncover
To you, who have been her lowly and fond lover,
Build humbly a high music from within
With pain and pleasure, righteousness and sin,
That shall not prove a merely jingling rhyme
To wheedle idle whimsies of the time,
Nor blared applause of idle fool to win,
Perishing with him ; uttered when you burn,
The world may welcome, or the world may spurn,
Uttered for love thereof, as in your prime,
The message you are commissioned to deliver,
If men will hear, well !—if not, to the Giver
Who breathes it through you will the word return.
Dare not to claim for self the utterance ;

One, out of His perfection, will advance
The same to stand His own ambassador,
Yea, full accomplish what He sent it for.
In other ways, moreover, look that thou
Serve men—help whom or want, or sorrow bow.'

His clear young tones, mine antidote to bane,
Methought resumed : I heard them once again.
' The God in us, with God who is in the world,
Perchance electeth from eternity
Time-process, evil relative, for ends
Of grander good, beyond us, absolute ;
But here we falter,
Grope darkling, and surmise with bated breath :
Yet our deep Best will justify the Lord :
How strengthen thews of any champion,
Save through the powerful antagonist ?
Civilizations only fall to ruin,
That richer may be reared from their decay ;
From chaos ever nobler order grows.
                                        Who repents
Hath God behind him, and the World-Idea,
To uplift him when he fails ; a mother holds
Her child, who falling, learns at length to walk.
Even that awful Shade, that made for Death,
Changing resolves itself to Life at length :
Trust only in the sound, strong Heart of all !
Nor only Reason, Love belongs to God :
Our Human sunders ; our Divine will blend.

Evil and good are complemental ; more
I know not ; but there is a Deep beyond,
In the Abysmal Spirit. . . .   Hide your eyes
Before the mystery of mysteries !' . . .
He shading his, that sought the Infinite,
I droop mine, blinded with the blaze of light :
Methought now all the innocent victim-blood
Streamed with the Lord's upon the holy rood :
I saw, and worshipped ; I believed in God. . . .

And then he vanished.   I awoke ; but earth
Was lighter than before for his sweet birth :
Winter without me, in my heart was spring,
Where all the happy birds began to sing."

POEMS.

TO MY MOTHER.

I AM weeping, mother, in your empty chamber;
Beyond the pane, a fair familiar scene;
As a far dream only may the man remember
All the mirth of childhood that hath been—
Hath been here about thy young joy, O my mother,
All the mirth and laughter of a child!
Was it I, indeed, and not another,
Whom you folded in your dear arms undefiled?
Our nursery with snowy-folded curtain!

You were wont to give me orange-petal candied,
From the china bird, laid yonder near the clock. . . .
Ah! visionary seasons, are ye banded
To weave illusion round me and to mock?
In the chestnut grove our nest, where in the leaf-
　　time
We children took our strawberries and tea,
Hath fallen; dove, and cuckoo here renew their brief
　　time,
Pale primrose, and the windflower, wood-anemone.
While I recall delightful days of childhood
In the home of our forefathers, when from school
I came to wander with you in the wild wood,
And my happiness ran over, very full.
How I lingered on the hard road in the damp night,
When you left me at my school, until aloof
I beheld no more your lessening line of lamplight,
Nor heard the minished trample of the hoof!
Among German forest-firs you tell the story,
As we go, her hand who died, and mine in yours
Ah! the bonfire on the hillside, and the glory
Of our rural meal among the bilberry bowers!
Then a cottage o'er a torrent-haunted valley
In the summer-sounding vines was our abode,
Where Morn and Eve upon the mount continually
Wrought a robe of glory, as for God.*

* Above the Rhone Valley; in sight of the Dent du Midi.

Yearly, later, on an evening of the winter weather,
With our youngest born who died we came to you :
On arrival, what a welcome, at the meal we ate
    together,
You gave to weans, and wife, and me, so tender and
    so true ! . . .
All our converse in my manhood ! by the healthful
    ocean-margin,
Or where we loved to hail the holy morning-glow,
Beyond blue water, on the mountain men have named
    the Virgin,*
On the glory of her heavenward height of pure and
    solemn snow.
In the isle where cloudy, melancholy Blaaven,
Of noble mould, empurpled, rules the heaving sea,
You, enfeebled, I supported from the haven,
To where Coruisk glooms crag-immured in lone
    sublimity. . . .
And the churchyard lieth beautiful to-day, love,
As in yonder dearer, earlier time,
When we wandered hand in hand with you in May,
    love,
We children, you in all your lovely prime !
Every green grave is a garden gently tended,
And birds sing in the orchard near the dead,
Meet repose for one whose day serenely ended,

* Beatenberg.

Very weary, when the saintly spirit fled !
Joy was yours, and yet your life knew much of
    anguish,
Disenchantment, weariness, and pain ;
In the later years of weakness, when I saw you
    languish,
I felt our aching void would be your gain.
Love unfailing, kindly counsel, all the pleasure
In your mere delightful presence, and your smile !
It is a loss that none may map or measure ;
Life will feel it every weary mile !
O you, who were so kind and so forgiving,
If I grieved you, how my heavy heart hath bled !
Ah ! and though unloyal hours may wrong the living,
We never think unkindly of the dead !
Friend in need, O consolation of the mourner,
Faithful heart, who suffered unremoved !
You leaned upon the Faithful, not a scorner ;
You loved well ; yea, and you were well-beloved.
A little lamb is playing in the orchard,
Faery gleams are fleeting on the hill ;
There is a breath of lilac in the churchyard,
And the dead are lying very still.
All the vernal loveliness a shadow
Of lovelier havens wherein you abide,
Cooler woodland water, warmer meadow,
In the love of Him, who healed you when you died !
Faded letters, and our pilgrimage in dreaming

Raise the dead, more dear than living men,
For, however we believe it only seeming,
Night brings them warm and real to our arms again !
It may be, mother mine, when you departed,
White and silent, that you did not wholly go,
Never left your children broken-hearted,
Help them more, are nearer than they know.
And your remembered tones are more than music,
More than day the memory of your smile ;
Clear from all the cadences of sorrow,
May I hear them, and behold them in a little while !
Our eldest, and our youngest, are they gone now ?
For a moment I may linger by the grave ;
It may be that my day is nearly done now ;
Lord, I would have them yonder ; heal, and save !

FOWEY.

WHERE the wooded hills enfold
A gleam of river water,
Luminous brown ripples hold
Communion of laughter,
Silent laughter with the trees,
Water-woven cadences,
Bole and foliage leaning over
The innumerable water-lover.
A weathered arch divinely hued,
With drowsy waterlight imbued,—
All the delicate semitones,
Purple, lilac, greys, and browns,
As tho' ineffable fine feeling
Over it were silent stealing—
Orbed to rondure in the stream;
Ah! ruffle not the glassy gleam,
Nor mar the fair unearthly dream! . . .
A rill babbles like a child
In the ear of flowers wild,
Who, nodding to the lucid lapse,

Quiver when the silver taps.;
Here a wheel revolving spills
Urgent weight of flashing rills,
To soft white flour bruises yields
Of the mellow autumn fields.
But another resteth near
All idly; this for many a year,
Urged by falling water's weight,
Toiled for human ends; of late,
Roofed by woodland leaves from sun,
It resteth, the long labour done,
Silent; little herbs and flowers
Have woven delicate green bowers
Over the well-travelled wheel,
Wont to grind our misty meal.
Blue germander, feathery grass,
Jewelled with a dewy glass,
Wild geranium, wood-sorrel,
Visited by moths like coral,
Azure butterflies, and bees,
Lush luxuriant herbs like these
The old water-wheel enwreathe
With a kind of verdure-sheath;
Even as a chrysalis,
Lapped in silent silken bliss;
To the toil-worn all may seem
Like a sweet long summer dream.
So a new-arrived saint,

World-weary, after the death-faint,
In the sleep wherewith Love bound her
Finds a lovely dream around her,
A radiant vision of repose
Involves her when her eyelids close.
　　Here the folding hills abide
Wooded to the water edge;
Many a leafy nook they hide,
Where, landing on a grassy ledge,
One may moor the boat and lie,
While leafy light and shadow play
With the rippling river nigh,
Where tall heron, of plumage grey,
Waits, or bluebird flasheth by;
Ample, warm, luxuriant light
Bathes in trance of deep delight,
Till the joy resembles pain,
And full eyes begin to rain.
Fair Lerrin hamlet, Ethy quay,
Your memories are dear to me,
Your murmured tones soothe memory!
St. Winnow's hoary old church tower
Drowses in a leafy bower,
While the waters gently steal
From the groves of Lostwithiel.
　　Now, rower, grapple with the wave!
Flood no longer smooth and suave,
Brown-ridged with feud of wind and tide,

For great ocean far and wide
Invades the river; swiftly glide,
Pass the orchard-nested village,
Fern, heath, pasture land, and tillage,
Pass the sounding woodland shore,
And vessel lading, till the oar
Be shipped in yonder ampler space
Near the battlements of Place.*
Whose the gleaming porphyry hall,
Near Fimbarrus † fair and tall;
There the lady of Treffry
Compelled besieging hosts to fly;
There bold gallants of the past
Marshalled many a seasoned mast,
Loosed the harbour chain, and met
The warrior King Plantagenet,
For irresistible advance
Upon the hostile coast of France.‡
A quaint old tottering house is here :
To the homely laddered pier
Fishers bring their haul to sell
Opal-hued, green mackerel,
Dry their nets, and gossip glad,
Blue-girt, big-booted, man or lad.

---

* The seat of the Treffry family.
† The Church of St. Fimbarrus.
‡ Carew says that Fowey sent forty-seven sail to assist
Edward III. in the siege of Calais.

How often our lithe oar-blades quiver
Upon the healthful tidal river!
How they round the guarding fort,
To find a well-beloved resort
On tawny sand along the coast,
Where huge rugged rocks are tost,
By caves, for some enrapturing bathe,
Where nought may interrupt or scathe;
Only green billows dance, and fly
White sea-mews with their dear wild cry.
O the tender-tinted lavers,
Where a dimpling water wavers,
Pink, purple, lilac; turquoise gems
Illume imbathèd amber stems.

Crimson weeds from ocean groves
Fleck the yellow floor of coves,
Diapered by gently-flowing
Ripple when no winds are blowing,
Memories of lace-like foam,
Where confused soft bubbles roam,
Launch forth a faery promontory,
Form momentary silver bays;
And when they vanish, heavenly glory
All the shining shore inlays,
A mirrored pure cerulean hue,
Fine fleeces floating in the blue.
Or by moonlight, how we drove
Our keel into a yielding cove!

Pale foam whispering on the sand,
Eerie as a goblin land,
Shadowy arch, and cave, and stone,
One phantasmal semitone;
Like visions wizard Wagner raises
With mystical enchanted phrases.

   O'er the harbour's pale expanse,
Resembling a profound death-trance,
Under a cold misty moon,
Fragments of an alien tune,
While with bated breath we float,
Are wafted from the anchored boat—
Choral singing, flute, or lyre;
The grey wave rolls a flickered fire
From her lit porthole; shadowy
Ships with phantom sail go by.
Hark! some rushing, throbbing sound
Of a steamer outward bound!
And baying of a far-off hound! . . .

   Beyond the harbour a dim-heaving sea
Breathes, awful with infinity;
Recalls the vanity of man,
His idle noise, his feeble span;
We are all children of the mighty Main!
Why fear to rest upon the Mother Heart again?
Launch forth, and sleep
Upon the deep!

THE MERRY-GO-ROUND.

THE merry-go-round, the merry-go-round, the merry-go-round at Fowey ! *

They whirl around, they gallop around, man, woman, and girl, and boy ;

They circle on wooden horses, white, black, brown, and bay,

To a loud monotonous tune that hath a trumpet bray.

All is dark where the circus stands on the narrow quay,

Save for its own yellow lamps, that illumine it brilliantly :

Painted purple and red, it pours a broad strong glow

Over an old-world house, with a pillared place below ;

For the floor of the building rests on bandy columns small,

And the bulging pile may, tottering, suddenly bury all.

But there upon wooden benches, hunched in the summer night,

Sit wrinkled sires of the village arow, whose hair is white ;

* Pronounce *Foy.*

They sit like the mummies of men, with a glare upon
    them cast
From a rushing flame of the living, like their own mad
    past.
They are watching the merry-make, and their face is
    very grave;
Over all are the silent stars! beyond, the cold grey
    wave.
And while I gaze on the galloping horses circling
    round,
The men caracoling up and down to a weird, monoto-
    nous sound,
I pass into a bewilderment, and marvel why they go;
It seems the earth revolving, with our vain to and fro!
For the young may be glad and eager, but some ride
    listlessly,
And the old look on with a weary, dull, and lifeless
    eye;
I know that in an hour the fair will all be gone;
Stars shining over a dreary void, the Deep have sound
    alone.
I gaze with orb suffused at human things that fly,
And I am lost in the wonder of our dim destiny. . . .
The merry-go-round, the merry-go-round, the merry-
    go-round at Fowey!
They whirl around, they gallop around, man, woman,
    and girl, and boy.

Q

"AH! LOVE YE ONE ANOTHER
WELL!"

Ah! love ye one another well,
For the hour will come
When one of you is lying dumb ;
Ye would give worlds then for a word,
That never may be heard ;
Ye would give worlds then for a glance,
That may be yours by ne'er a chance ;
Ah! love ye one another well !

For if ye wrung a tear,
Like molten iron it will sear ;
The look that proved you were unkind
With hot remorse will blind ;
And though you pray to be forgiven,
How will ye know that ye are shriven ?
Ah! love ye one another well !

"LOST ANGEL."

Lost angel of a holier youth,
O maiden fair beyond compare !
Young dream of joy, return for ruth,
Dawn, breathe around a holier air !
Evanished where?
Dear naiad, in a shadowy grot,
Fair nymph, who lave within the cave,
I yearn for you, and find you not,
O freshness of the early wave !
The river rolleth broad and strong,
Great vessels glide upon the tide,
High storied tower and temple throng
With human toil, and pain, and pride.
But where the purple light of morn,
And thou, fair queen of what hath been?
Ah ! holy land where Hope was born,
Ah ! freshness of the early green !
O shrined within the lucent air,
Where Youth hath birth with morning mirth,
Clear-welling crystal blithe and fair,

Leaf-mirror from the loins of earth !
But I am drifting far away,
With many a stain, with many a pain,
I near the shadowy death of day,
And youth may never dawn again.
O grand cathedral where you prayed,
Divinely dight with jewelled light,
Soft woodland water where we played,
Low music in the summer night !
Melodiously flowing river !
Ah ! blithe sunshine upon the Rhine,
We would have leaned, and looked for ever,
Your eyes more luminous, lady mine !
Dark as a russet forest pool,
With many a dream within their gleam,
Now glancing mirth, now veiled and full ;
Were they, or did they only seem ? . . .
There is no grove like yonder grove,
No water clear as our mild mere,
No dawn is like the dawn of love,
Nor any later flower so dear
As are the earliest of the year. . . .
Evanished where ? . . .
Holds life, or death, immense and still,
Thee darkly fair beyond compare ?
May Love her silver orb fulfil
Unhindered there,
Where Honour may not fetter will,

Nor Love Himself bid love despair?
And you were one long vernal kiss,
Immingling glows of lovelit rose,
Perfume, rare amber, ambergris,
And all the fervid Orient knows!
Ah! mellow-ripe-of-autumn hue,
Young, willowy, warm, impassioned form,
Tone gentler than the turtle-coo,
Brown eyes that took the heart by storm,
And lovelier inward grace that drew
My soul with all-compelling charm!

"*I LOVE YOU, DEAR!*"

I LOVE you, dear, and we must part,
Although your heart be on my heart!
I love thee, though thou art not mine ;
I love ; yet I may ne'er be thine!
And will our passion ne'er be fed,
But wait, and wither, and lie dead?
Alas! it seems a world made ill,
Where poor love may not find her fill!

"HANDS THAT WANDER."

HANDS that wander o'er the keys,
Lithe hands over ivory keys,
I remember hands like these
Flying over ivory keys
In the far-away dim years,
I remember them with tears;
They were wont to rest in mine
In the early morning-shine,
And I wonder where they are;
Very, very far!
If I ever came too near,
I have prayed, God save you, dear;
Heaven gave your griefs and blisses,
Holds in whatsoe'er abysses.
You, who were my dearest friend,
I loved, I love you to the end!
What have we to equal love
Here in earth, or heaven above?

Maiden of the clear brown eyes,
Where no sin nor sorrow lies,
I love thee for thy melodies,
And for thine innocent deep eyes.
In the far-away dim years,
May they rarely cloud with tears!
True and clear as now they are
Keep them, Heaven, when I am far!
I shall never come too near,
Only pray, God save thee, dear!
Guide in all thy griefs and blisses,
Hold thee in the deep abysses!
Ye who claim the name of friend,
Love one another to the end!
Have we aught to equal Love,
Or in earth, or heaven above?

THE LITTLE IMBECILE.

A MAN slow climbed a wooded hill ;
An idiot boy was mounting too,
Before him ; near, and nearer still
The elder gradually drew.
The boy paused often looking back ;
His knees were tremulous and bent ;
With large vague eyes along the track,
Upon a sound he seemed intent.
He crooned out " Waggon " o'er and o'er,
For he could hear one far below,
Then turning mounted as before,
His weary footsteps planting slow !
The man appeared oppressed with care,
Gloomy, sin-burdened, and distraught ;
He mused, " The little pilgrim there
Was born by accident, for nought !
Yea, what avails the vacant life,
A mere grim burden unto kin ?
Yet he eludes the bitter strife,
The wounded heart, the tyrant sin ! "

And now that they are near abreast,
The elder feels a sudden hand
Laid boldly in his own to rest,
A quiet, unashamed demand
For kindly help; the boy who tires
Prefers unhesitating claim
On whom unreasoned faith inspires
To feel a friend, without the name.
The man supports the smiling child
With pleased amazement; hear him cry—
" Forgive me, dear, if I defiled
Thine innocence with calumny !
Yet I for whom affection fails,
Who fail to others, wildered roam,
Am leaned on by the child who ails,
Who sees, confides, and feels at home.
I love thee for the confidence,
That lightens and sustains my heart ;
Through muffling mists, though ne'er so dense,
God's glory gleameth, when they part !
White wings of Ruth embowered above,
Her breathing spheres thee like an air ;
Unfathomable maternal love
Rebukes the ravings of despair.
Thou quickenest dead hearts to bleed,
And poor grey listless lives to live ;
My blessing on the gentle need,
Unlocks the miser hand to give,

Compels the barren womb to breed,
Moves Heaven a damned soul to forgive !
No uses ! were it only this !
I see that all things have an end ;
The boy hath innocence and bliss,
Yea, higher help himself may lend,
Which will be known to him for his.
Remove thy shoes, adore, and bend ;
Around are holy mysteries ! "

ARISE !

A Song of Labour*

From the long sleep of centuries,
   Rise, arise !
Ye will be men at last, not slaves,
From your cradles to your graves ;
   Life is dawning in your eyes ;
      Arise !

Weary children of the soil,
   Who toil and toil !
Patient millions of night,
Turn worn faces to the light,
   Piteous hunger in dim eyes,
      Arise !

Miserable, dumb, and blind,
   Of humankind !
With divinest discontent
Stony souls at last are rent,

* Written on the formation of Unions for agricultural labourers.

Human souls immersed and bowed
In the dark dull earth ye ploughed !
From brute suffering ye break ;
       Awake !

Murmur men who rule you, scared :
      " What ! ye dared,
Doltish bovine bondsmen, ye !
To claim, with accents of the free,
   For yourselves, and babes, and wives,
      Human lives !"

Mummied princeling of the past,
      Ecclesiast,
Shopman, overshadowing shires,
Dining delegates, and squires,
   A moneyed mob aghast and pale,
      Rant and rail :

Who told you? let him drown for this,
   With our bliss !
We, though we leave you ignorant,
Lest ye behold a yawning want,
   Doled you gracious doles, and gave
   Ghostly cheer to keep you brave ;
   Yea, paupers, and we dug your grave !
      Ye rave !"

Stalwart, sturdy sons of toil,
   Ne'er recoil !
Dare they threaten violence?
Form your phalanx deep and dense !
What though tyrants always cry,
When God consumes their tyranny,
" Dare not rouse you from your swound ;
Heaven's order ye confound !"
   Never fear ; be calm, be wise !
   Holy fire inflame your eyes !
   God shall smite your enemies :
      Arise !

A CASUAL SONG.

SHE sang of lovers met to play
"Under the may bloom, under the may,"
But when I sought her face so fair,
I found the set face of Despair.

She sang of woodland leaves in spring,
And joy of young love dallying;
But her young eyes were all one moan,
And Death weighed on her heart like stone.

I could not ask, I know not now,
The story of that mournful brow;
It haunts me as it haunted then,
A flash from fire of hellbound men.

THE CHILD'S JOURNEY.

A LITTLE child at morning-tide
　　Was journeying by train ;
She saw the shining landscape glide
　　By the clear window-pane.

Tall trees, fair village, and green field,
　　Blithe boys with bat and ball,
Church spire and meadowed kine appealed
　　To eyes that answer all.

Blue-frocked, by her fond mother, she
　　Embraced a doll in red,
And when she dined, full tenderly
　　The faded doll she fed.

The trains flew by with fleecy steam
　　That melted in the blue ;
But when there sloped the westering beam,
　　Weary the maiden grew.

And when the mother fond compels
  With wisdom more than hers,
The weary little heart rebels,
  The childish anger stirs.

With feeble hand she strikes her mother,
  Who gravely kind reproves ;
And now the child her grief would smother,
  Upon the heart that loves.

The parent folds her little maid
  More closely to her breast ;
Upon her own the child hath laid
  Her doll, and sinks to rest.

I wonder if the Heart of all,
  Whence our poor hearts arise,
Be more unpitying when we fall,
  From being wholly wise ?

THE TRUE KING.

AZURE waters lapt in light,
To folds of gleaming, widening blue,
Parted by the prow's swift flight,
Soft simmered as we lightly flew;
A mile-long lane of foam we left;
White winging birds the clear air cleft.
A princely boy of Eastern blood,
Swathed all in silk-inwoven gold,
Of royal mien, with joy imbued,
A form of finely-chiselled mould,
Played upon the deck well-kept,
Watched the flying fish that leapt.
An English dame addressed the child
"Shall I tell you of the Lord,
"We English love?"   He sweetly smiled,
And blithely took from her the word
(From some white nurse he may have heard)
"I'll tell *you* /   He was gentle, mild;
"None see Him, though they try to find;
"Yet He is here ! but like the wind.

" Though Jesus Christ a king was born,
" Men put on Him no real crown,
" They made Him wear one all of thorn ! "
" Nay, none more real e'er was known,
" Than that by which His brows were torn,"
She answered, " Your ancestral gem
" Burns low beside that diadem !
" The purple robe of Night He wears,
" Starred over with the world's wild tears,
" Was dyed in His own harmless blood,
" Whose throne imperial was the rood.
" No rival royalty Love fears ;
" Who spends Himself for all is king ;
" He hath you under His wide wing ! "
The large eyes wonder, and grow grave
A moment ; then he runs to play,
To note the glancing of the wave,
Or the red pennon flicker gay.
But in far years, mid pomps so brave
Of yon resplendent Indian court,
And dangerous homage dark men brought,
A hallowing on his heart there lay
From that meek lesson which she taught.

THE MONTH OF THE NIGHTINGALE.

I.

It was in the month of the nightingale,
I found my love !
Flowing with rivers of light in the vale,
Haunting a heart of moonlight pale,
The bird o'erflowed ;
Or in the dusk of his green abode
A cuckoo vied
With the lovesong tide,
And with a lark's divine delight
In a fountainous, azure-imbathèd flight :
We lay and listened, I and my love,
We lay and listened in the grove ;
Butterflies blue
Merrily flew
Over wood-sorrel dewy wet ;
Mossed windflower and violet
Thrilled in the air, and our lips met :
From under a shade of sunny boughs

We saw the green blade sprout in the brown
Field fallows, and far haze of the town,
Cattle in misty water-meadow browze,
And young lambs play
In far fields of May.
All the young happiness of spring
Supremely flowered, burst forth, took wing,
In two young hearts to sing,
In two young lovers, in our own love,
Pure and happy as the saints above !

II.

Now in the month of the nightingale
I have lost my love !
And I heed no more the tender tale,
But I hear the sorrow in a flute-like wail
Deliciously complain ;
No pain to him,
No sorrow to the bird in his covert dim ;
Only foreboding of a human pain,
Searing hearts to a barren plain,
When we find the love we deemed immortal
Only death's flower-enwoven portal !
And we wander alone,
In a desolate land alone, alone,
Hearing a dove's low, soft love-moan,
Among primroses and young buds,
Where cresses waver in the clear spring floods.

I know not how Love faints away,
And with him all the bloom from day,
And with him all divine delight
From dull unconsecrated night ;
I know not how Love dies, nor how he is born;
I know my life is left forlorn.

RETURNING THANKS.

I THANK Thee, Lord, I may enjoy
Thy holy sacrament of Spring!
For dancing heart when leaflets toy,
Or when birds warble, and wave wing,
For tears, for April tears of joy!
The cuckoo thrills me as of yore,
The nightingale is more than wine;
Bluebells in the wild woodland pour
Hues purpler, but not more Divine
Than blithe, fresh hues of Heaven on high;
I thank Thee, Lord, before I die!
Sidelong glance, brown rabbit furry,
Ere to foot-patted hole you hurry,
Under large leaf, rumpled, shady,
By a folded lord or lady!
Anemone, and pale primrose
Already gone! in place of those,
Blue speedwell, purple violet,
With the dews of morning wet.
These innocent pleasures never cloy;

I thank Thee, Lord, I may enjoy!
Pure, fresh scents pervade the wood,
A dim, life-teeming solitude;
Young juices mount, and gums exude!
Our children in dear days long fled
Pulled daisy, and sleek golden cup;
One left us, and men deem him dead;
And two have well fulfilled our hope;
And all by Thee, my Lord, are led!
I lie upon the woodland green,
With sorrel, little strawberry flower;
Through pink wild apple-bloom sun-sheen
Plays hide-and-seek, in the lush bower
Of murmurous leaves, and hour by hour
Makes shine and shade for the soft flower,
While birds unbosom love's young glee,
Dallying round the nested tree;
For I, and all, are dear to Thee!
How long since I was a blithe boy!
Much went with youth's removing wing;
But, Lord, I thank Thee I enjoy
As then, Thy sacrament of Spring!

THE POLISH MOTHER.

A Dramatic Monologue.*

SHE looked a matron from the ancient world
Of Roman grandeur, tall, pale, proud, black-robed.
Strong passion chained, with poignant suffering,
Held down by stern hand, crouched, yet writhed alive
In her fine countenance; whose graven lines,
White hair, death-pallor, and deep caverned eyes,
That lustrous burned with fierce intensity,
All prophesied the death-doom imminent.
She was a Pole of ancient lineage,
Whose son, Count Român, made a prisoner
In those great hopeless battles, which the race
Fought, for the right to be, with the strong Tzar,
Had been condemned to labour in the mines
Of far Siberia perpetually.
  Now she conferred with one, whom suffocation
Of all free thought and speech in Russia made

* Founded on a real incident, mentioned by Liszt in his "Life
of Chopin."

Wild to wrest freedom by main force, a lady,
Young, fair, fanatical ; to whom she told
The story of the wrongs, that wrung consent from her
To violent counsels of conspiracy.
    "I could not kneel; my knees were turned to
        marble ;
I could not save my son, my only child !
And yet you know well how I loved him ! how
I had waited for him, tended from the birth,
Fed from my own life's fountain ; when he ailed,
Bent over, watching wakeful by the bed,
Hearing him breathe, and soothed when he awoke.
Myself I ministered to want and whim ;
My being hung on his ; my thoughts returned
Thither, however far afield they flew,
Hovered around him, birds about the nest.
Ah ! boy beloved, my heart's home was in thee !
    Hours of our early love, the balmy moons
By drowsy, lisping seas in the warm south,
Were they more dear than later summer evenings,
When, after favourite tale, accompanied
By rippling laughter from my baby boy,
Mother undressed him (nurse had holiday,
Sweet birds were warbling, the young rose was blown)?
We sang our simple songs, dear, you and I,
Until you only crooned them, half in dream,
Then softly glided into slumberland,
Away from mother ; but her heart still held you !

'Where is he now?   In some profounder sleep.
Where is he now? . . . they say I might have saved
    him.
I was too proud.   My God ! I might have knelt !
There was one moment only—I could not !
    My son, the count, fought like a patriot Pole
Against our old hereditary foe.
Made captive, Nicholas himself had added,
When signing the imperial decree
Of lifelong death in far Siberian mine,
Whence none emergeth more to social day,
' Thither shall he go manacled, on foot.'
Ha ! do you know what that means ? 'chained, on
    foot '?
It means to tramp long winter through to summer,
Athwart interminable steppes, and snow,
To that bleak outcast region beyond hope,
With one coarse convict yoked a bondfellow,
Defiled in body, and defiled in mind,
With him to tramp, to feed, to lie by night,
Subject to every brutal outrage from
Soldiers who love to wreak indignity
Upon one outlawed, of high grade, refined :
And if his strength (but he was weak, and ailing)
Sustained through that dread journey to the goal,
Live burial in the nether deeps of earth,
Toil so repulsive, so interminable,
That men have killed their guard, to win the grace

Of being knouted to a speedier death—
Or else malignant years, that beat men down,
Each with his own peculiar stroke, combine
Here their slow malice into one supreme
Assault, and turn the young man deaf, blind, grey,
Quench in a year the fading faculties,
Render imbecile ere the very end.
Or men escape in winter weather; then
They may lie down, and faint out in the snow. . . .
And this was he who lay upon my breast,
And drew warm life I stored up there for him—
For whom I would have parted with all mine. . . .
Why, then, did I not save him? why? God knows!
If God there be—but when the tyrant came,
An evil sneer upon his curving lips,
My knees were turned to stone; I could not move—
Kneel to the insolent murderer of my people,
Who now would torture my poor child, in wrath,
Because he paid his country what he owed her—
You know not the conditions the man made,
Indignities designed to break my pride—
To break the pride of Poland—of one born
Illustrious as any emperor.
On such conditions, if I craved for pardon,
(Pardon forsooth! and mercy! and from him!),
He would toss me the freedom of my child,
Contemptuously as you toss bone to dog—
Exemption from his own injustice, his

Inhuman sentence—nay, there is a God!
This man must needs be punished for his life!
These degradations I refused; for honour
Is more than life; more even than one's child.
At last, the Empress, pitying me, arranged
That I should ask an audience of her;
Then he the autocrat would cross the room,
And I upon my knees might crave for grace. . . .
He entered, while we talked; I never moved.
So she, supposing that I knew him not,
Rose, and I rose too; but he slowly passed,
Staring, incarnate Insult, in mine eyes,
The stare of arrogant autocracy,
With sneer that relished our humiliation.
He slowly passed, looked, lingered, and went out.
The Empress seized my two hands, and she cried:
'You have lost your only opportunity!'
    Face to face with the murderer of my country,
I was the daughter of Poland, and no mother!
In that brief moment I beheld *my* Mother,
Poland, my Mother,
Dishonoured, and dismembered; felt them part
Her frame, yet warm, assigned among three tyrants. . . .
What did I see?   I saw in vivid vision
Our green fields bloodied, corpses in the woods
Of fair, brave brothers—felt them beaten to death
By Tartar soldiers, maddening in dungeons
Deprived of day, dank, loathsome, for the love

They bore our common Mother ; saw corn, food
Trampled by hooves barbarian, crushed down
Under the mangled bodies of her sons ;
The flaming smoke rolled up from ruined homes,
And women sobbing on the unroofed, wrecked
    hearths—
And not one heart, but multitudes of hearts,
True hearts—lay broken in the mines of hell ! . . .
What did I hear?   I heard the syllables
We loved to lisp in childhood on loved knees,
Silenced for ever among living men,
Forbidden to be spoken by the children. . . .
Ah ! ah ! the children ! wailing they were dragged,
Dragged from mad mothers' arms, and heaped in
    waggons,
Jolted along the frozen snows, for nurse
The brutal Cossack, cursing when they cried,
Their mothers following the dwindling carts,
And floundering into snowdrifts ; happy they,
If to remain there ! while the children's cry
Dwindled to silence ; all became so still ! . . .
Supreme stroke this of cynic cruelty—
Infants torn from their native land, to learn
Upon an alien soil from mortal foe
Forgetfulness of our parental love,
Indifference to their people's agony,
That so young Polish hearts might ossify
To Russian ! trained to arms for their oppressor

Young Poles made Russian soldiers, and degraded,
Cajoled by demons to abjure themselves. . . .
Seeing and hearing which, how could I kneel
To him, in whom our injury was summed,
And centred ; radiated, from a deadly sun ?
I could not kneel, not even to save my child. . . .
But I am going to Român ; all is well ;
If not to meet him, then to rest in sleep.
He sleeps, he rests now. Very soon I with him.
Ah ! so is best ! much better than if Time
Slackened the close clasp of Love's fingers, ere,
Wearying of His mumbling fools, He broke
   them. . . .
And vengeance only slumbers : work your will
Upon the tyrant ! I will help ; take gold :
Earth will be cleaner for one stain wiped out."

PRINTED BY WILLIAM CLOWES AND SONS, LIMITED, LONDON AND BECCLES.